A BOTTLED CHERRY ANGEL

'All right. So I'll be Peter and you can be Wendy.
And now that I know where you live, Wendy, I
might come and visit you some time. P'raps tonight, if I feel like it. Shall I come tonight?'

'I – ' She was on the point of saying that tonight,
if he really meant night, and not just after school,
wouldn't be convenient since she had her homework to do and anyway Mrs Jenkinson would never
let her go out to play in the dark, specially not with
a strange boy, and anyway she didn't know that she
wanted him to come and visit her. After all, she
didn't like boys.

A Bottled
Cherry Angel

Jean Ure

BEAVER BOOKS

A Beaver Book
Published by Arrow Books Limited
62-65 Chandos Place, London WC2N 4NW

An imprint of Century Hutchinson Limited

London Melbourne Sydney Auckland
Johannesburg and agencies throughout
the world

First published by Hutchinson Children's Books 1986
Beaver edition 1987
Reprinted 1988

Text © Jean Ure 1986

Printed and bound in Great Britain by
Anchor Brendon Limited, Tiptree, Essex

ISBN 0 09 951370 6

1

'Really, Samantha!' Miss Jenkinson paused, exasperated, in her task of correcting IIIB's class work. 'How many more times must you be told? I-before-e-except-after-c . . . that is the rule!'

In red felt tip, very angry, Miss Jenkinson slashed through the word 'recieve'. *RecEIve*, she wrote. *Remember!!!*

'I shall have to give you a D− for this piece of work. It is quite a disgrace and I am most upset and put out by it.'

Samantha Potter, she wrote, in the book where she kept the weekly marks. *D−*. She pushed her spectacles up her nose with the middle finger of her left hand and sternly surveyed Samantha through them.

'What have you to say for yourself?'

Samantha only stared woodenly and said nothing.

'Stupid child!' said Miss Jenkinson. She turned to the next exercise on the pile. Her expression grew softer. 'Carlotta Fitzmaurice . . . excellent! Not one single mistake – and so beautifully written! I shall give you an A+.'

Carlotta had had nothing but A+s since the beginning of term. (She was Miss Jenkinson's favourite, which probably wasn't fair but couldn't be helped: teachers always had favourites.)

'Tamsin Alexander . . . B. You can do better than this, Tamsin, if you try. I am afraid that you are rather lazy. Tiffany Johnson! Not a lot of imagination, my dear, but quite a good effort. I think perhaps B—. Louise Sc—'

All of a sudden, Miss Jenkinson froze.

What was that?

She strained her ears, listening. A harsh grinding sound, followed by a clunk ... then the scrunch, scrunch of footsteps, making their way over gravel.

Miss Jenkinson left her seat and flew across to the window. Through a chink in the curtain she peered out. Too late! Whoever it was had already reached the porch, was already rat-tat-tatting with the polished brass knocker.

Miss Jenkinson turned and ran to the door. (IIIB remained where they were, stolid, blank-faced, staring straight ahead.) With her ear to the crack, Miss Jenkinson could just make out the sound of voices. And then just one voice, louder than the rest: 'Midge! Someone for you!'

In something like panic, Miss Jenkinson whirled back across the room. One by one she began snatching up IIIB and flinging them into the depths of her wardrobe. Samantha, Louise, Tiffany, Tamsin, Alexandra, Teresa ... pell mell, they were all hurled in. (She hurled Carlotta last, because Carlotta was her favourite and she wouldn't want her to be crushed.) She just had time to slam and lock the wardrobe door and sweep all the exercise books into the old tin trunk which she kept under her bed before the door was thrown open and the horde burst in. Actually there were only two of them but they seemed like a horde, all fresh and cold from the outside world and making lots of noise.

'What on earth are you up to?' shrieked Emma.

'You're looking all guilty,' said Match. 'Have you been doing something you oughtn't?'

'No,' said Midge, wriggling.

'I bet you have!'

'I haven't,' said Midge.

'She has, she has!' Match flung herself exultantly on to

6

the bed, bouncing up and down on it as if it were a trampoline. 'She's been up to naughties, all by herself!'

'What was it?' said Emma, curious. 'Was it something rude?'

'Or were you smoking ciggies?'

'Course I wasn't.' Midge flicked a plait over her shoulder and pushed up her glasses with the middle finger of her left hand. She could feel herself going all silly and poppy-coloured. 'I was reading.'

'Reading what? Something dirty?'

'No!'

'So why're you all embarrassed?'

'I'm not all embarrassed! What d'you want, anyway?'

'What d'you want, anyway?' Match mimicked her, as she trampolined up and down. '*That's* not very polite.'

It wasn't very polite to come bursting into someone's bedroom and start bouncing on their bed and accusing them of reading something dirty.

'We're going into town,' said Emma, 'to look round the shops. You coming?'

'All right.' She had really been quite happy shut away by herself marking IIIB's exercises, but if Match and Emma were going into town then there could be no question of Midge not going with them. They always did things together. They always had done, right from Juniors. The three Ms, they were known as: Midge, Match and Emma. (Originally, terms and terms ago, they had been Midge, Match and Moo-cow, shortened to Mooc, on account of a singing teacher once informing Emma that she had a voice like a sick cow, but Emma had very soon decided that Mooc wasn't dignified, especially for someone who had naturally curly hair and pretensions to beauty.)

'It's going to snow,' announced Match, still trampolining.

'Goody, that means we can use my new sledge.' And

bother, she had gone and locked her jacket in the wardrobe. She didn't dare to get it out with Match and Emma looking on; not with the whole of IIIB hidden away in there. She would just have to wear the dirty old anorak which hung in the hall.

'Your mother', said Emma, 'said that you were *doing* things.'

'Reading's doing things.'

'She made it sound as if you were doing other things.'

'Playing with her dollies,' suggested Match, trampolining nearly up to the ceiling.

Midge, down on hands and knees by the side of the bed, scuffled in the gloom for a pair of shoes.

'Oh, but Midge and Matchstick *love* their dollies,' carolled Emma, happily, in Mrs Jenkinson's voice. 'D'you remember your mother saying that?' She bent and addressed Midge, underneath the bed. 'You and Match were cross as hornets!'

'That was yonks ago,' said Match. She bounced herself upright. 'Look here, are we going into town or aren't we?'

On their way out through the front door they bumped into Midge's sister Sue on her way in with her latest boyfriend, who was foreign and wore a ring in his ear and was called Rawl. Sue took one look at Midge in her old dirty anorak and screeched, 'For goodness' sake! Do you have to? You look like something off a rubbish tip!' Match and Emma both giggled.

'I don't know how you can bear to be seen out with her. Go back and put something decent on!'

'Can't be bothered,' said Midge.

'You're repulsive,' said Sue. 'Do you know that? You are actually *repulsive!*'

Match and Emma giggled again: Midge just stuck her hands in her pockets and stumped on. She was used to Sue telling her she was repulsive. (Repulsive, repugnant, revolting, repellent....) Sometimes Mr Jenkinson would try to stick up for Midge and tell Sue to 'stop picking on the child', but Mrs Jenkinson just said it was the difference in their ages.

'Was that your sister's boyfriend?' Emma wanted to know.

Midge grunted.

'Is he Italian?'

'Dunno.' Something foreign, that was all she knew. Match and Emma were always asking questions about Sue's boyfriends. How old is he? What's he do? Where'd she meet him? Midge could never understand what it was they found so fascinating.

'What's his name?'

'Rawl.'

'*Rawl?*'

''swhat it sounded like.'

There was a pause.

'Rawl's a funny name,' said Emma.

'Prob'ly isn't Rawl.' Match took a long-legged leap across two cracks in the pavement. 'You know what she's like.'

'It's prob'ly Pietro,' said Emma. 'He looks like a Pietro.'

'D'you think people *do* look like their names?'

'Sometimes they do.'

'Do I?' said Match.

Emma studied her a while. 'D'you mean, d'you look like a match?'

'No, I mean', Match spoke rather breathlessly, 'do I look like an Antonia?'

'Not really,' said Emma. 'But I expect that's 'cos we're too used to calling you Match.'

'Yes; that's what I thought.'

9

Match frowned and with great deliberation began treading from crack to crack. Midge, humping along with her hands in her pockets, wondered how long it would be before it started to snow, so that they could go up to Bethany Hill and use her new sledge. Last year, when it had snowed hugely and tremendously for days on end, all they'd had was an old plastic dog bed which kept catching on things and overturning. Now she had her lovely new sledge and not a single drop of snow had they seen all winter.

'I'll tell you what!' Match suddenly twirled round, dramatically, to face them. 'I've come to a decision.'

''bout what?'

''bout names.'

'What about them?'

'I have decided,' said Match, 'that I don't think people ought to go round calling me Match any more.'

Not call her Match any more? What was she talking about? Match had been Match for as long as anyone could remember.

'Well, anyway,' said Match, 'that's what I think.'

'So what d'you want people to call you?' Emma sounded interested; almost sympathetic. 'D'you want them to call you Antonia?'

'I thought maybe . . . Toni?'

'Ye-e-es.' Emma nodded, considering it. 'Yes, Toni's nice! I like Toni. All right, we'll call you Toni.'

Midge was staring, accusingly.

'We can't do that!'

'Why can't we?'

'If we call her Toni, we won't be the three Ms any more!' Even when Emma had stopped being Mooc they had still been the three Ms – after all, you couldn't get much more M-ish than Emma.

'We haven't been the three Ms for *ages!*' There was a hint

of impatience in Emma's voice. 'Where've you been living? Under a stone?'

Midge felt her cheeks go poppy-coloured again. Match looked at her, kindly.

'It was all right for Juniors.'

'Some people,' said Emma, 'oughtn't ever to have *left* Juniors if you ask me.'

Midge swallowed.

'P'raps we ought to start calling her Flora,' said Match.

'I don't want to be called Flora!' Flora was horrid: Flora was a grandmother name.

'No, and anyway,' said Emma, 'she's still a midget so she's got to be Midge. Let's go into Morgan's and look at the lanjery.'

They had only recently discovered the lanjery. It was where the underclothes were kept, all the knickers and slips and bras. (It was actually spelt lingerie, and for a while that was how they had pronounced it until Sue had overheard them and nearly died laughing.) Midge didn't really enjoy going round the lanjery, especially with Match and Emma in one of their more showing-off moods, keeping on giggling and fingering the goods and talking about cup sizes.

'Why don't we do hats?' she said. She liked doing hats. You could try them on, and look at yourself in the mirrors.

'We did hats last week. I'm sick of hats.'

'Well, joolry, then.'

'Can't do joolry.' Match giggled. 'We did joolry on Wednesday after school with Alison Soper and she went and broke a whole string of beads, treading on them . . . they said if they ever saw us there again they'd report us.'

Midge fell silent. She hadn't known that Match and Emma did things with Alison Soper. Alison Soper hadn't

11

even been at Juniors with them. Last term, when they'd started at Hazelgrove High, Emma had decreed that she was 'above herself' and oughtn't to be spoken to, and as a matter of fact Midge never *had* spoken to her. Now the others were going round Morgan's with her after school, trying on the jewellery.

Midge trailed disconsolately across the store behind them to the escalators. (Where had *she* been, last Wednesday after school? She hadn't been anywhere. She'd gone straight home and done her geography homework and set up a maths test for IIIB.)

The lanjery department was on the first floor, past Electrical Goods and through Toys. When they had been *really* little (say five, or six, or seven) Toys had been the most wonderful place on earth, but of course one was above all that sort of thing now. That sort of thing was for Juniors and Infants. When you were a Senior you grew out of toys. You went to look at the lanjery, instead, and talk about cup sizes.

'What I want to know –' Match shouted it excitedly, across a store full of people '– is how you find out what you are?'

'You measure,' said Emma. Her voice held the ring of authority: Emma knew about things like measuring. 'First you measure underneath, then you measure round the tips—'

'Round the *tips?*' said Match. She giggled.

'And then when you've done that you take one away from the other and what you're left with is the cup size.'

'But how d'you *know?*'

'They have these charts,' said Emma. 'Like with tights. Of course, if you tried measuring *her* –' she gestured at Midge, '– you'd prob'ly get a minus.'

Midge scowled. So what? Sooner be a minus than a great

12

fat plus, all wibbling and wobbling and flopping about. Tits were horrible; she didn't ever want any. Sometimes, locked away in Emma's bedroom, Match and Emma would undo their blouses and eagerly examine themselves in the mirror for signs of growth. Midge always had to do it too, but what Match and Emma didn't realize was that Midge was checking herself for signs of flatness. If she started to stick out even just the tiniest littlest bit she would *die*.

She hunched her shoulders in her old dirty anorak. When she got home she was going to finish marking IIIB's essays, then when she'd done that she could add up all the results since the beginning of term and see who was top. Well, she knew who was *top*, Carlotta was top, she always made her the cleverest, just as she always made her score the most runs at rounders and have the longest rallies at wall tennis, but it would be fun to find out who was next. One time it had actually turned out to be that stupid Samantha. *That* was something that wasn't going to happen again.

She suddenly became aware of Match's voice shouting exultantly in her ear: 'Marian Cooper's are absolutely huge!'

They were talking about tits. In *public*. And on a Saturday afternoon, with the store crammed just about as full as a store could be.

'Sophie Westmore's hardly got any at all.'

'Nor's Tracey Harris.'

'*Or* Jennifer Barlow ... Jennifer Barlow's flat as a pancake.'

Heavens! They were going through the entire sixth form. Midge sunk herself down, as deep as she could go, into the depths of her anorak. She felt quite sick with embarrassment. All the Saturday afternoon shoppers were turning to stare (and some of them were *men*).

'Stovey's are nice,' said Match.

'Stovey's are super.'

'What size d'you think Stovey is?'

'Mm . . . 'bout thirty-six.'

'Thirty-six B or thirty-six C?'

'Thirty-six B.'

'That's the size I'd like to be,' said Match. 'I wouldn't want to be all big and flobby like that girl with the moustache.'

'Karen Angelis. She's about a forty *D*.'

'Imagine what she must look like when she has a bath!'

Midge kept her gaze fixed firmly on her shoes. School shoes. Brown, with laces; thick for winter warmth. Match and Emma wouldn't wear their school shoes at weekends, just like they wouldn't wear their school blazers. They said that the shoes were clumpy and the blazers were drear. Midge didn't terribly care about clumpiness, and actually she quite liked her blazer. You could stick your hands deep into the pockets and drag them down, and you could pin badges on the lapels, and—

'What are you *doing?*' She found herself being jabbed, rather irritably, in the ribs. 'Are you in a *trance*, or something?'

'Must be the knickers,' said Match. She giggled. 'It gets some people like that.'

Slowly Midge raised her gaze from the floor and discovered that she was standing directly in front of a table covered in frilly underwear. She *hated* the lanjery department. She wasn't ever going to come into it again.

'If you would just kindly move,' said Emma, giving her a shove, 'we could go up to the next floor.'

The next floor wasn't so bad. It housed the self-service cafeteria, where you could get Coca Cola and potato crisps and pink meringue shells filled with chocolate. There was also a ladies' cloakroom with machines that blew hot air and interesting messages written on the lavatory walls, sometimes about people that one knew. A few weeks ago Midge had discovered one about a girl at school called Sandra Green. The message had said, SANDRA GREEN IS A OAR. They had puzzled and puzzled over it, until in the end Emma had deputed Midge to go and ask Sue, since Sue had once been in the same class as Sandra Green and therefore ought to know. Midge had been reluctant – 'It might be something rude!' – but Emma had said that that was all the more reason for finding out, and why couldn't Midge just do as she was told?

Emma could be very bossy at times; there wasn't really any arguing with her. Midge had approached Sue, but cautiously.

'You know the word "oar"?'

'Yes.' Sue had been instantly suspicious. 'Is this a trick?'

'No! I want to know.'

'Want to know what?'

'Well, you know it means a thing for rowing a boat with?'

'Yes.'

'Does it mean anything else?'

'What sort of anything else?'

'Well, like if I said someone was one.'

'If you said someone was an oar?'

'*A* oar,' had said Midge, quoting. 'So-and-so is a oar.'

Sue had looked at her, rather hard.

'You'd just better hadn't!'

'You mean,' Emma had grumbled later, 'you didn't ask her what it *meant?*'

Match had groaned: 'Trust her!'

There weren't any interesting messages today; only someone called Elspeth saying that she loved someone called Stevie. They racked their brains but couldn't think of a single solitary person they knew that was called Elspeth.

'Stevie could be Steven,' said Match. She glanced slyly sideways at Emma as she said it. Midge, watching, was surprised to see Emma's nice pink-and-white complexion turn slowly brick colour. That was very odd: Emma almost never blushed.

'D'you like the name Steven?' said Match. She seemed to be addressing the question to Midge.

'Not specially,' said Midge.

'*She* does. It's her favourite.'

'Shut up, it isn't!' said Emma. 'And anyway, if I like Steven, then you like Darren.'

'*Do* you?' said Midge. She thought Darren was a perfectly horrid name.

'Yes, she does,' said Emma, at exactly the same moment as Match said, 'No, I don't.'

'Yes, you do! Don't lie!'

'I'm not lying, I *don't*. I think Darren's *foul*.'

'That's not what you thought last week!'

'Yes, it is!'

'No, it isn't!'

'Yes, it is!'

'No, it—'

'Paul's nice,' said Midge. 'My aunt's new baby's called Paul.'

There was a silence, then: '*Paul!*' said Match.

'Goo-goo-goo,' said Emma, plopping her finger in and out of her mouth.

They giggled. Not for the first time Midge found herself quite unable to see what it was they were laughing at.

2

'Ugh!' Sue catapulted her chair back from the breakfast table with a clatter. Face contorted, she glared at Midge. 'Do you always have to be so foul and disgusting? Look at you – look at the mess! It's revolting!'

Midge, unmoved, went on dipping toast fingers into her egg. Mr Jenkinson reached across for the teapot.

'Stop getting at the child.'

'I'm not getting at her! She's getting at *me* – I shall be sick in a minute! Great gobbets of egg yolk all over the place . . . it's like having breakfast with an animal!' Sue turned, and appealed to her mother. 'Can't she be shut away in the garage or something?'

'What?' Mrs Jenkinson, as usual, was buried in her newspaper. She wouldn't have cared, or even probably noticed, if Midge had eaten her breakfast upside down and hanging from the lampshade. 'You know, it really is quite outrageous–' the pages of the paper rustled angrily '– the way the press distorts things. Look at this headline!' She flashed it briefly at them, across the milk jug. ' "CND MARCH TAKEN OVER BY COMMUNIST RABBLE" There wasn't any rabble! I *know* – I was *there!* It was as orderly as could be. This is pure right-wing propaganda.'

Silence. Mr Jenkinson lifted the lid off the teapot and peered, without too much hope, inside it. Midge chomped stolidly on a finger of toast.

'As for *Com*munists—'

'Never mind Communists,' said Sue. She said it with bitterness and loathing. 'What about *her*? At least I bet Communists don't slurp egg yolk all over the place when they eat.'

'Communists don't have egg yolks,' said Mr Jenkinson. He winked. 'Can't afford 'em.'

Slowly and dangerously Mrs Jenkinson lowered her paper.

'Would you mind repeating that?'

'Certainly!' Mr Jenkinson grinned, slyly, into the teapot. 'I said, Communists don't have egg yolks, they can't afford them.'

'I bet if they *could* afford them they wouldn't eat them in that disgusting manner.'

'Well, of course they can afford them! Don't be so ridiculous.'

'It's repulsive,' said Sue. 'Why can't it grow up? I mean, look at it . . . egg all over its face – and *plaits*.'

'What's wrong with plaits?' Mr Jenkinson wanted to know. 'I'd wear plaits if I could only grow my hair long enough.'

Since Mr Jenkinson had started going prematurely bald at the age of thirty-three, this was obviously intended as a joke. Sue, however, like Mrs Jenkinson, didn't always see when things were funny.

'It's just so *childish*,' she said. 'Like wearing socks – what's it still wearing socks for? Nobody wears socks when they get to senior school!'

'Yes, they do,' said Midge. 'Pearl Chillery does.'

'And who in the name of all that's wonderful is Pearl Chillery?'

'Girl in my class.'

'A girl in her class that wears socks.'

'And she has plaits,' said Midge. 'Dozens of them.'

18

'Dozens of them!' Mr Jenkinson relayed it triumphantly to Sue. 'So beat that if you can!'

Sue tossed her head.

'She's probably black.'

'Yes, she is.'

'Well, there you are, then! That doesn't count.'

'What do you mean, "that doesn't count"?' Mrs Jenkinson looked round, sharply, from her newspaper. 'I hope you're not being racist?'

'For crying out *loud!*' said Sue.

At school that morning, in the cloakroom, Midge found Match and Emma sitting on the radiator together, giggling and somewhat self-consciously swinging their legs.

'What have you done to your skirts?' said Midge. She had to look twice before she could see that they were wearing any.

'Shortened them,' said Emma. She slid off the radiator, adopting a pose, arms in the air, hip stuck out. 'Like it?'

Midge stared, dubiously. There seemed to be an awful lot of leg – and Emma's legs were not the most elegant. As a matter of fact they were rather short and pudgy.

'Did you ask your mother?' she said.

Emma looked at Match: they giggled.

'Didn't need to ask her!'

'But won't she be mad?' Even Mrs Jenkinson, who in general didn't bother getting mad about the ordinary, everyday things of life, such as accidentally burning down the garden shed or chucking red ink across the sitting-room floor, would probably be a bit peeved at the thought of Midge chopping her one and only school skirt practically in half. It mightn't rate quite as high as right-wing propaganda against CND, but she wouldn't be too happy

19

about it – and Emma's mother was ever so much more fussy than Midge's. 'What's she going to say when she finds out?'

'Ha ha!' said Emma. She did a little twirl. 'Who knows?'

Match giggled, and slid off the radiator.

'I can see almost right up to your bottom when you do that,' said Midge.

'So what?' Emma, becoming brazen, pulled her skirt even higher and did the splits on the cloakroom floor. (Tried to do the splits on the cloakroom floor: Emma wasn't really what you would call athletic.) 'She's wearing tights, isn't she?'

'And anyway,' said Match, 'it's not as if there's any boys around.'

'Imagine if there were!' Emma, from her sprawling position on the floor, flung out both arms in a melodramatic gesture. 'Darren, oh Darren—'

'Shut up!' said Match, giggling.

'Toni, oh Toni—'

Match, still giggling, bashed at Emma with her school bag.

'Swoon!' said Emma, keeling over.

There were times, just lately, when Midge really didn't know what to make of Match and Emma.

On the way upstairs to the assembly hall (and if you were at the foot of the stairs and Match and Emma were at the top you *would* be able to see their bottoms, which even in tights was still pretty rude) they ran into a twittering knot of fellow first-years. The knot unravelled itself, and there in the midst was Alison Soper, with her skirt even shorter than Match and Emma's. Match and Emma didn't seem in the least surprised that Alison Soper should have chosen to lop half a metre off her skirt on exactly the same day as they had done so. Alison Soper didn't seem surprised, either. She simply looked at them and giggled and said, 'I didn't think you'd dare!' Midge knew, then, that it was something they had secretly planned.

'You wait till Miss Kershaw sees you,' said Pearl Chillery. 'You won't half cop it.'

The didn't exactly cop it, because Miss Kershaw wasn't the sort of person to make people cop it, she was far too nice, but certainly her eyebrows rose when she saw them in Assembly. She signalled at them, frowning, from across the hall, pulling at her own skirt as a sign that they should do something. She obviously didn't realize, thought Midge, that they had gone and taken the scissors to them. It was too late, now, to do anything. Their mothers were going to be *furious*.

All through Assembly heads were craning, people giggling. Members of the sixth form, sitting on the platform with Miss Turnbull, had a front seat view. Some of them, like Jennifer Barlow (flat as a pancake) looked sour and disapproving; others, such as Marian Cooper (absolutely *huge*) and Barbara Stovewell, known as Stovey, seemed to be having difficulty keeping a straight face. Midge was almost certain she saw Stovey's lips start to break into a grin. Miss Turnbull, fortunately, was hidden away behind her reading desk and couldn't see. If she had been able to she would probably have stopped Assembly there and then like she had last term when a girl called Veronica Beasley had come into school with her hair dyed purple.

'We do not have purple hair, Veronica, at Hazelgrove High.'

She had said it in front of the whole Assembly, all cold and cutting. Miss Kershaw wasn't like that, perhaps because she was younger (or perhaps because she wasn't a head mistress). All Miss Kershaw said, quite pleasantly, as she prepared to take the attendance register back in the classroom, was: 'I'm sorry, you three! I have nothing what-

soever against shortskirts as such, especially –' with a sort
of twinkle in the direction of Match '–if someone happens
to have the legs for them, but I'm afraid I really can't allow
it to be right or proper for the classroom. So, if you
wouldn't mind just readjusting yourselves—'

'But Miss Kershaw,' said Alison, 'short skirts are in
fashion!'

'They were in fashion years ago, Alison, when I was your
age – and I remember my teacher telling me exactly what
I'm telling you now . . . there is a time and a place for
everything, and school is definitely *not* the place for running around half naked. So come on now, roll down those
waist bands!'

Midge stared, in amazement, as with groans and protests
three skirts were restored to normal length. So they *hadn't*
taken the scissors to them, after all! She'd wondered why
Match was looking rather bulkier than usual round the
waist. (She hadn't wondered about Emma because Emma,
though pretty, was undeniably a pudge.)

'Did you wear mini skirts, Miss Kershaw, when you were
young?' That was Alison Soper, being cheeky.

'I did indeed,' said Miss Kershaw. 'But not to school!'

'Do you wear them now? *Out* of school?'

'Good gracious, no! At my age?'

'But you said, that if someone has legs worth dis-
playing . . .'

Everyone knew that Miss Kershaw had the legs: she had
played, last term, in the staff versus sixth form netball
match, dashing up and down the court in a pair of bottle
green shorts far shorter than a mere mini skirt.

An interesting blush spread over Miss Kershaw's
cheeks. (Fancy a teacher, *blushing*.)

'Legs or not, my dear Alison,' she said, 'one cannot
remain a Peter Pan for ever. There comes a time when we
all of us have to face up to the unpalatable truth. You're

looking worried, Pearl! Have I said something that gives you a problem?'

'What's a peter pan?' said Pearl.

'What's a Peter Pan? You mean to tell me you really don't know?' Pearl shook her head, with its dozens of plaits. Miss Kershaw laid down her pen. 'Is there anybody else who doesn't know?'

A girl called Trisha Walters, who never knew anything, promptly stuck up her hand. After a second or so a few more rather waveringly followed suit, Emma's and Alison Soper's amongst them.

'Well!' said Miss Kershaw. 'This is a sorry state of affairs! Lorraine, *you* ought to know.'

She only said that because Lorraine's aunt worked in a library; Lorraine didn't really know any more about books than anyone else. Last year when they had had a quiz it had been Midge who had come out top, not Lorraine. All the same, Midge was glad Miss Kershaw had asked someone else because although of course she had *heard* of Peter Pan (even dead ignorant people like Trisha Walters must have heard of him) she wasn't absolutely one hundred per cent certain that she knew who he was. Not exactly.

It seemed that Lorraine wasn't, either.

'Was it someone in a play?' she said, hopefully.

Miss Kershaw nodded. 'Yes?'

'Someone that didn't want to grow up?'

'Yes?'

'That's all I know,' said Lorraine.

'So who can help us out?' said Miss Kershaw. 'Caroline? Flora? Someone must be able to!'

Caroline Monahan volunteered the information that she had once had a book called *Peter Pan* when she was very young, only she couldn't now remember anything about it except that she had had a nose bleed over it and all the pages had got stuck together.

Tracey Nicholls then said that she had seen the play (when *she* was very young) and that it was about a family called Darling that was looked after by an old English sheepdog, and there was a girl called Wendy who had two brothers called John and Michael, and Peter Pan was a boy who was dressed in sort of rag things and came flying in at the window and took them all off with him to somewhere called the Never Never Land where there were Red Indians and pirates and some Lost Boys without any parents, and there was a crocodile that had swallowed an alarm clock and wanted to get the pirate captain, who was called Captain Hook because of having a hook instead of a hand, and the crocodile hated Captain Hook, and so did Peter Pan, and Peter Pan and Captain Hook had a battle, which Peter Pan won, and Wendy cooked all the meals and kept house and looked after everyone (*groans*) until in the end she decided it was time to go home and so they all flew back again except for Peter Pan, who stayed behind in the Never Land.

'By himself?' said Midge.

'Yes,' said Tracey, 'because the Lost Boys had gone back with the others' ('*Boo! Shame!*') 'and were going to be adopted, and go to school' ('*Horrible!*') 'and live with the Darlings.'

'So what happened to Peter Pan?'

'Dunno.' Tracey looked vague. 'I s'pose he just stayed in the Never Land on his own.'

'Sounds dopey to me,' said Alison.

'It's not in the least bit dopey! It's a children's classic,' said Miss Kershaw, 'and I'm horrified that you're all so ignorant. We shall obviously have to do something to remedy the situation. I'm sure there must be a copy of the book in the school library . . . who'd like to volunteer to go and get it out and read it for us? Emma?'

Emma pulled a face: she never went near the school library if she could help it.

24

'No!' said Miss Kershaw. 'I can see the idea quite obviously does not appeal. Emma would sooner read about pop stars . . . I daresay if the truth were known you would all sooner read about pop stars?'

General giggling, and nodding of heads.

'Is there not one single person who would like to read about Peter Pan?'

'I'd like to,' said Midge.

Some of the giggling increased: some of it turned to groans.

'Trust her!' said Alison Soper.

Midge couldn't find *Peter Pan* in the school library. To begin with she didn't know who it was written by and had to ask Tracey Harris, the prefect in charge. Tracey Harris snapped, 'J. M. Barrie! Don't they teach you people anything these days?' Then when she looked on the shelves under B it wasn't there, which meant that Tracey had to come and look as well, which made her cross because Tracey was studying for a university scholarship and considered herself above having to cater for the infantile needs of mere first years.

'It's probably got put back in the wrong place. Either that or it's been stolen. Anyway, *Peter Pan* is kids' stuff. Why can't you read something worthwhile? Dickens, or something?'

'Don't want to read Dickens.' She wanted to read *Peter Pan*.

'Well, you'll just have to go on looking,' said Tracey. 'It's your own fault. If you won't put things back where they belong—'

'But I never took it out!'

'Well, *some*one did.'

Midge stood, mutinous. Prefects were so unfair, always

blaming other people. Emma said it was because they were too big for their boots, but Tracey Harris wasn't big, she was all weedy and shrivelled. Stovey, on the other hand, who was what Mrs Jenkinson called well-built (and what Mr Jenkinson called 'strapping') was as fair as could be. If Stovey had been in charge she would have gone through every book on the shelves.

'I'll come back later,' said Midge. Stovey might be there later. 'I haven't got time to look now.'

'Suit yourself.' Tracey shrugged. 'Why you can't read something *decent* . . . I'd read practically the whole of Jane Austen by the time I was your age.'

Midge wrinkled her nose. They'd done some Jane Austen last term with Miss Kershaw. It was all about grown-ups falling in love with each other, and she couldn't see there was anything very interesting in *that*.

'Still, of course, if you can't even be bothered to look,' said Tracey.

It wasn't that she couldn't be bothered, it was that she had to go and play in a hockey match, Under-13s versus Under-14s, to see who was going to be chosen for the Junior XI. She and Match were the only two people from the first year to be in the Under-13s. Match, who played left wing, had been picked because she had the longest legs of practically anyone in the school and could even out-run some of the fifth and sixth formers in the First XI. Midge, who was centre half, had been picked for her nuisance value: she might not have long legs but she could zoom in and out and get in people's way and generally unsettle them.

'Like a nasty little wasp!' Emma had once declared crossly, in a hockey lesson, when Midge had nipped in front of her, and Emma, in her clumsy fashion, had tripped over her hockey stick and come down *thump* in the mud. Emma loathed hockey. She loathed netball and gym as well, but

26

she loathed hockey more than anything.

As they walked across to the field together, scrunching in their hockey boots over the frosty grass (it was going to snow any day now, the weather man had forecast it) Match said: 'I found out what a oar is.'

'What is it?'

'It's a woman that stands on the pavement in a fur coat and talks to men.'

Midge's eyes grew round.

'What would she do that for?'

'They get paid for it.'

'For standing on the pavement?'

'For talking to men.'

Midge wrestled a moment with the image. Mrs Reed up the road had a fur coat. She quite often stood on the pavement and talked to men. She had been talking to Mr Jenkinson only the other day.

'Who pays them?'

'The men do.'

'Just for *talking?*'

'No, stupid! For other things.'

'What other things?'

Match looked mysterious.

'*You* know.'

There was a pause.

'What people do,' said Match.

Midge rubbed a finger up her nose.

'How d'you find out?'

'Alison Soper told us. Last night, at the Youth Club.'

'You went to the Youth Club?'

'Yeah, it's smashing. There's table tennis and a disco and –' Match turned a bit pinkish '– and boys and everything. You ought to come sometime.'

Midge swished with her hockey stick.

'Don't like boys.'

'No, that's what Emma said. I said why don't we ask Midge, and she said it's no use asking *her*, she—' Match suddenly stopped. Her cheeks, which had been pale pink, grew slowly scarlet. 'Look, there's Stovey!'

Midge looked. Match had a thing about Stovey. Midge didn't exactly have a thing – at least, she didn't think it was a thing. She didn't blush whenever Stovey looked at her (which was possibly because Stovey never did look at her) and she didn't hide round corners, giggling, just to catch secret glimpses, but if there was one member of the sixth form whom she would most like to have had as a big sister (in place of Sue) then it had to be Stovey. She felt sure Stovey wouldn't always nag at her and jeer at her and tell her she was repulsive.

'Horrors!' squeaked Match. 'She's going to stay and watch!'

It certainly seemed as if that were Stovey's intention. She was standing on the sidelines, quite close to Alison and Emma ('Lucky pigs!' said Match) with her stripey sixth form scarf wound about her neck, her hands thrust into the pockets of her navy duffle coat. Match had turned the colour of a boiled beetroot. Midge felt quite sorry for her. How awful to be so gone on someone! It was like having the measles and breaking out into spots.

Midge didn't break out into spots but she couldn't help being aware that Stovey was there, at the side of the field, watching every move. Stovey herself played centre forward for the First XI, so it had to be assumed that she would watch the centre players more than she would the wings. Midge zipped and zoomed even more busily than usual. One good thing about it was that it did at least take her mind off Match and Emma going to the Youth Club with Alison Soper. That was one of the meanest things they had ever done. *It's no use asking HER*. Emma was getting really beastly since she'd started talking to Alison Soper.

The Under-14s beat the Under-13s by five goals to nil, which wasn't really as much of a disgrace as it sounded since the Under-14s had all been playing for at least two years. Stovey stayed right to the end. She had been joined by horrid shrivelly Tracey Harris, who perhaps wasn't quite so horrid as she seemed because as Midge came off the field she shouted over to her: 'Here! You! *Peter Pan!*'

'*Peter Pan?*' said Stovey. She sounded impressed. And, 'Oh, good catch!' she added, as the book was lobbed across.

Midge beamed. Hugging *Peter Pan* to her chest, she trotted after the others.

'She talked to you!' hissed Match.

'She's been talking all the time.' Alison reached out and snatched at *Peter Pan*. 'Let's have a look.'

'Cor! Fairies!' said Emma.

'I know a fairy.' Alison sniggered. 'Lives down our road.'

'There's one in here called *Tinker*bell,' said Emma, craning.

'One down our road's called Clarence,' said Alison. She and Emma giggled. Match, looking a bit uncertain, gave a little half-hearted snicker. 'He's not really,' said Alison. 'He's called Tim, but my Dad calls him Clarence 'cos he walks like this.'

She took a few mincing steps, waggling her bottom as she did so. This time Match giggled as well as Emma.

'Here, cop this lot!' said Alison. She began reading out loud from the book. '*He was a lovely boy*—' ('Ooh! Lovely boy!' carolled Emma) '—*clad in skeleton leaves and the juices that ooze out of trees.*' ('Ugh! Yuk!') '*But the most entrancing thing*

29

about him was that he had all his first teeth, and when he saw that she was a grown-up . . .', Alison paused for effect, *'. . . he gnashed the little pearls at her.'*

Emma screamed. She and Alison staggered against each other, limp with laughter.

'Give it here!' said Midge. 'It's mine!'

'Give it here!' mocked Alison. 'It's mine!' She tossed the book at Midge (who this time didn't catch it and had to scrabble ignominiously for it on the ground). 'Load of mush!'

'It's not mush.' Miss Kershaw didn't think it was mush. Nor did Stovey. Stovey had sounded quite impressed.

'It's dribble,' said Alison. 'It's for babies.'

'Didn't you hear Stovey?' said Emma. ' "*Peter PAN?*" She must think you're retarded or something.'

'She thinks she's a bottled fruit,' said Alison. She and Emma giggled again.

'What d'you mean, a bottled fruit?' Carefully Midge wiped the cover of *Peter Pan* on the sleeve of her hockey sweater.

'It's what she said,' said Alison. 'She was talking to Tracey Harris and she said, Flora looks just like a little bottled fruit.'

'Bottled cherry, *ac*tually.'

'She said I looked like a bottled cherry?'

'I s'pose you do, a bit.' Match studied her a moment, head to one side. 'Sort of round and – and cherrylike.' And then, kindly: 'It's quite a nice thing to be, really. Imagine if she's said a bottled cabbage.'

'Yes, or a pickled walnut.'

Midge couldn't help feeling that she would rather Stovey hadn't said anything at all.

3

On Friday morning, at the end of English, Miss Kershaw said: 'How are you getting on with *Peter Pan*, Flora? Did you manage to find it in the library?'

'Yes.' Midge flicked a plait back over her shoulder. 'But I haven't actually started it yet.'

It was still in her desk, safely hidden beneath a pile of text books. Every time she went to take it out she thought of Stovey calling her a bottled cherry.

'Well, when you do,' said Miss Kershaw, 'just try and remember that it was written at a time when girls of eleven were very much more innocent than they are now. There was no television, no cinema, no video – some of them even still believed in fairies. Yes, I know, Alison! It is amusing, isn't it? But we're not talking about that kind of fairy. That's a very good example of what I mean when I say that Edwardian girls were innocent . . . they would not have had the least idea what Alison was sniggering at.'

Midge wasn't too sure that she had much idea, either. Alison was always sniggering at things she couldn't understand.

'No eleven-year-old of Barrie's day,' said Miss Kershaw, 'would ever, for instance, have had a boyfriend; not in the way you people have.' (*Boos, jeers, cries of 'Shame!'*) 'And they would certainly never have had crushes on pop stars – well, of course there weren't any pop stars. If they were going to

31

have a crush on anyone, it would most likely have been the school hockey captain.'

Titters. Sly glances in the direction of Match, who had turned scarlet. (Stovey mightn't be hockey captain, but she did play for the First XI.)

'So, just bear it in mind, Flora, when you start the book. Try to put yourself in the place of an eleven-year-old girl living at the turn of the century – 1904, to be exact. Who was on the throne in 1904? Does anybody know?'

Someone said, 'King George V?' Someone else said, 'Queen Victoria?'

'Edward VII,' said Miss Kershaw. 'Which is why we call it the Edwardian era. In fact, it might be rather a good idea, when Flora's read the book, if we were to do a project on it. Flora could tell us about *Peter Pan*, and what it was like to be a child living then; the rest of you could take other subjects . . . politics, education, fashion . . . you could try asking at home, see if your parents have any photographs. There must be plenty lying around in old tin trunks. Yes!' Miss Kershaw gathered up her books. 'I like it! We'll work on that idea.'

'Now see what you've gone and done.' Emma looked resentfully at Midge as Miss Kershaw left the room. 'Trust you!'

'Wasn't my fault,' said Midge.

'Yes, it was . . . saying you'd read her soppy old *Peter Pan*.'

'Someone had to,' said Match.

'So why's it have to be her?'

'Don't really see that it matters who it is,' said Match; but Emma, with a toss of her head, had already gone swishing from the room.

'What's her problem?' demanded Pearl.

'She's just in a mood,' said Match, ''cos she wanted stripes put in her hair and her mother wouldn't let her.'

'*Stripes?*' said Midge, startled. 'Like on a zebra?' Emma really was becoming most awfully odd.

'Must be bonkers,' said Pearl.

Midge threw back the lid of her desk. It was a relief to know she wasn't the only one who thought so. Encouraged, she twitched aside *Junior Maths I* and *Physical Geography* and snatched a quick peep at *Peter Pan*. On the cover was a picture of a boy with tousled hair wearing a raggedy kind of shirt and no shoes. He was standing on a bit of rock blowing what looked like a horn.

'What's she want stripes for?'

'Girl at the Youth Club's got them, 'cept hers are pink and green. Emma wanted hers mauve.'

'Raving nutter,' said Pearl.

Midge, growing bold, took *Peter Pan* out of her desk and studied the picture more closely.

'Is that it?' Pearl peered over her shoulder. 'Looks like a statue.'

Midge turned to the first page.

'"Statue of Peter Pan in Kensington Gardens." Where's Kensington Gardens?'

'London,' said Match. 'It's near Hyde Park. I went there last year when my Dad took us up to the Tower.'

'Did you see it?'

'What, the Tower?'

'The statue, you idiot,' said Pearl.

'What statue?'

Pearl looked across at Midge and rolled her eyes.

'There were thousands of people there,' said Match. 'You had to queue for hours to get in. There wasn't time to see everything. Look, are you coming –' she addressed herself sternly to Midge '– or are you going to stuff in here all break?'

'I'm coming.' Midge dropped *Peter Pan* back in her desk, banged down the lid and hurried over to join Match.

It was always Match, these days, who waited for her; never Emma. As they walked up the corridor towards the playground they could see Emma already going through the outer door with Alison Soper. Midge screwed her face up into a scowl. 'What's she got all friendly with her all of a sudden for?'

'I don't think she's *that* friendly,' said Match. 'Not like she is with us. At least . . .' she paused, considering, '. . . I s'pose she is *quite*. But it's sort of different, if you know what I mean.'

'Can't think what she sees in her,' grumbled Midge.

Match giggled.

'You ought to come along to the Youth Club!'

'Why?'

'Then you'd see her brother . . . then you'd know.'

'Know what?' (And what brother? *Emma's* brother? Emma didn't have a brother, she was an only child.)

'Know what it is that she sees.'

'In Alison Soper?'

Match giggled again. 'In her brother!'

'Alison *Soper's* brother?' Alison Soper's brother had come to the school play at the end of last term. Midge remembered him quite clearly. A horrible, loutish boy with long black hair all greasy and lank. Steven Soper, his name was.

'Hasn't she shown you?' said Match. 'She's got this chain round her neck with a big S-for-Steven on it.'

Emma hadn't shown her, and Midge had never noticed. Just lately there seemed to be more and more things she wasn't noticing.

'D'you go to the Youth Club quite often?'

Match nodded, enthusiastically. 'Go once a week.'

'On Sundays?'

'Sometimes it's Sundays. Sometimes it's Saturdays. Depends what's on. We're going Saturday this week . . .

Saturday evening. They've got this disco.'

Once upon a time on Saturday evenings they had gone round to one another's houses and had tea together and played games, and sometimes even stayed the night, all three of them crammed into the same bed, giggling and telling stories and not getting to sleep until the early hours. It was a long time since they had last done that. Midge couldn't imagine, now, lying in bed giggling with Emma. They didn't seem to giggle at the same sort of things any more.

Emma and Alison were walking round the playground, arm in arm. Alison had hair just like her brother, all long and lank and greasy.

'You could come if you wanted,' said Match. 'But I don't really think you'd go for it. Not if you don't like boys.'

'No, I don't,' said Midge. There was a boy next door called Damian Gilchrist who was nearly thirteen and was always trying to make her stop and have conversations. She hated him. (Sue kept calling him 'your boy friend', which made her hate him even more.)

'I mean, you can if you *want*,' said Match. 'It's just that it seems rather silly, if you're not going to enjoy it. And if you really don't like boys—'

She *hated* boys.

They walked for a few moments in silence.

'Let's catch the others up,' said Match.

Match took off, legs flying, across the playground. Midge stayed where she was, frowning ferociously just in case anyone was watching. The other day in the lavatories she had overheard Lorraine Peters talking to Caroline Monahan when they hadn't known she was there. Lorraine had said, 'If I invite Match and Emma, do I have to invite Midge Jenkinson as well?' and Caroline had said, 'No, she's not part of them any more. They go round with Alison Soper now.'

Midge flicked back her plaits. What did she care if they went round with Alison Soper? What did she care if they were all going to their stupid disco at their stupid youth club to drool over boys? She had better things to do. She had *Peter Pan* to read. She would read it aloud with IIIB, she decided; and when she had read it she would set them an essay to write, just to make sure that they had understood it.

'Now remember', said Miss Jenkinson, 'that this book was written a very long time ago when there wasn't any radio or television and nobody had crushes on pop stars and girls of eleven were still innocent and believed in fairies – please don't snigger like that, Samantha, it's extremely foolish. Thank you. Now, I want you all to pretend that you're living in the year 1904, which is the year that this book was written. Who was on the throne in 1904? Does anybody know? King Edward VII. That's quite right, Carlotta. Would you like to be the one to start reading for us? And just remember, please, Samantha, that we don't want any giggling. We are young ladies of the Edwardian times and we do not giggle. Very well, Carlotta.'

She chose Carlotta first because Carlotta had the best reading voice. (She always kept Samantha until last because Samantha was so stupid she stumbled over every second word.)

'Let us start at the beginning. This is called Chapter 1, Peter Breaks Through. Please begin, Carlotta. "All children except one . . ." '

' "All children except one" ', read Carlotta, in a voice remarkably akin to Miss Jenkinson's own, ' "grow up. They soon know that they will grow up, and the way Wendy knew was this. One day when she was two years old she was playing in a garden, and she plucked a flower and ran with it to her mother. I suppose she must have looked rather delightful for Mrs Darling put her hand to her heart and cried, 'Oh, why can't you remain like this for ever!' This was all that passed between them on the subject, but henceforth Wendy knew that she must grow up. You always know after you are two. Two is the beginning of the end." '

(Was it? wondered Midge. She couldn't even remember when she was two; at least, she didn't think she could. Perhaps later, when she was in bed, she would try very hard and see if she could think back that far.)

'Thank you, Carlotta.' Miss Jenkinson turned over to page 2. 'Who is next? Is it you, Tiffany?'

Tiffany had a high, tinkling sort of voice which was rather annoying, but she read quite well. After Tiffany came Tamsin, who couldn't pronounce her s's (and kept saying things like nurthery instead of nursery and meathleth for measles), and after Tamsin came Teresa, who had an Irish accent on account of being Irish, and then Louise, who was refined and spoke like a news reader on the BBC, and Alexandra, who was a bit dim, though not nearly as dim as Samantha, who was dimmer than absolutely anybody.

They had got halfway down page 9, where Peter Pan comes flying in through the nursery window, when the class was brutally interrupted by Miss Jenkinson's elder sister hammering on the door with her fist and shouting, 'Oy! What are you up to?'

Miss Jenkinson grew crimson.

'Not up to anything!'

And even if she was, it was none of Sue's business. Sue's bedroom, which was next door, had a large notice stuck on it saying *Visitors kindly Knock before Entering*. Midge's, rather more bluntly, had a notice which said *PRIVATE. KEEP OUT*. And in smaller letters underneath, *Trespassers will be Prosecuted*. Generally it served very well to keep other members of the family at bay; now, to Midge's fury and indignation, the door actually opened a crack and Sue's head dared to peer round.

'What's going on?' said Sue, curious.

With a shriek of rage, Midge hurled herself across the room.

'Go away! This is private property! You're trespassing!'

Sue, taking not the slightest bit of notice, stuck her head even further round the door.

'I thought I heard you talking . . . who were you talking to?'

'Nobody! Get out!'

'You're not still playing with your *dolls?*' said Sue.

'No! It's a project for school, go away!'

'All right, all right!' Sue backed out, on to the landing. 'You don't have to yell, I was only taking a friendly interest. *I* don't care if you want to play with your dolls. Ma and Pa have just gone off to CND, by the way. Rawl'll be here in a minute. D'you want to come down and watch television with us?'

Midge shook her head.

'You can if you want. We don't mind you being there.'

She didn't want to be there. It embarrassed her seeing Sue and Rawl sitting on the sofa holding hands and slurping over each other. And she bet they did mind, really. They were only having to stay in because of her; because Mr and Mrs Jenkinson had gone to CND and Midge was considered too young to be left in the house by herself. *She* wouldn't have had any objection to being left by herself. At least then she could have read *Peter Pan* in peace and quiet, without people peering round the door and spying on her.

'Why aren't you out with your mates?' said Sue.

'What mates?'

'Those two you used to knock around with . . . the little fat blonde and the one with the legs.'

"Cos I told you,' said Midge, 'I'm *doing* things. I've got to read the whole of *Peter Pan* for Miss Kershaw.'

'Well, if you change your mind,' said Sue, 'you know where to find us.' From down below came the sound of knocking. 'That'll be Rawl! I must go and let him in.'

Sue sprang off, down the stairs. Midge closed her bedroom door and turned back again to IIIB.

'Now, where were we?' she said.

Silence.

'Who can tell us where we were?'

No response; even Carlotta sat stupid and blank. It was always the same after someone had intruded: IIIB stopped being IIIB and became simply a row of lifeless dummies. Midge knew from experience that it was useless trying to do anything with them. Once they had gone, no amount of coaxing would bring them back.

'All right, children, that will be enough for today. You have worked quite hard. You may put your books away now and go for your break. Please leave the room quietly, without any jostling.'

One by one – Tiffany, Tamsin, Teresa, Louise, Alexandra, Samantha, Carlotta – she put IIIB away in the bottom of the wardrobe. The cuckoo in her cuckoo clock, which had been her eighth birthday present and came all the way from Switzerland, suddenly shot out at the end of his spring and cuckooed twelve times. That meant that it was almost half-past seven (the cuckoo being four and a half hours ahead of himself). She wondered what Match and Emma were doing at the Youth Club. Having a disco, Match had said. Midge had never been to a disco, though of course she had seen them on television, with everybody whirling about and jumping up and down and waggling their elbows. It wasn't too late to change her mind and go there even now, except that she wasn't absolutely certain where it was and maybe she would wear the wrong sort of clothes and say the wrong sort of things and then they would laugh at her and Emma would groan and say 'Trust her!' And anyway, there were *boys*.

Midge tiptoed to the door, opened it the tiniest bit and stood listening. From downstairs came the sound of gunfire from the television. Just as well Mrs Jenkinson wasn't here, she didn't approve of films where there were guns and shooting and people being violent.

Midge crept to the head of the landing and peered down, into the hall. The door of the sitting-room was firmly closed. That meant they were smooching together on the sofa.

Swiftly she stole down the stairs, crept past the closed door (definite sounds of smooching, in between the gunfire) snatched a packet of crisps, an oatmeal crunchy bar and an apple from the kitchen and scampered back upstairs to the safety of her bedroom. Who wanted to go to a mouldy old disco anyway? It was far more fun reading *Peter Pan*.

When Mr and Mrs Jenkinson came back from CND, Midge was still reading. She had finished her packet of crisps and her oatmeal crunchy bar and her apple, and had very nearly (but not quite) finished *Peter Pan*.

'Good heavens, young lady!' Mr Jenkinson – after knocking first and waiting to be invited: he was always very polite – inserted his head round the bedroom door. 'Isn't it about time you were asleep?'

'I'm reading,' said Midge.

'I can see that you are! But it's nearly midnight.'

'Can't I just finish this last chapter?'

'Well . . .' Mr Jenkinson looked over his shoulder for guidance.

'What's the book?' Mrs Jenkinson came into the room.

She was the one who decided. 'What are you reading?'

Midge held it out.

'Oh! *Peter Pan!* That's all right.' Mrs Jenkinson never minded Midge staying up if she were doing something that she approved of. 'I remember seeing *Peter Pan* in the theatre. Absolutely magical! All that flying! A bit blood-thirsty, of course, what with the Pirates and the Red Indians and everything.'

'Not to mention', said Mr Jenkinson, 'the crocodile.'

'Yes! I'd forgotten the crocodile! The one that swallowed the alarm clock . . . what happens to it?'

'It eats Captain Hook,' said Midge.

'Violence, you see.' Mr Jenkinson nodded. 'Violence, whichever way you turn.'

'Yes, but children *are* violent—'

Midge, curled up beneath the bedclothes in a nice warm nest, wriggled her toes. If her parents were going to set off one one of their voyages of discovery, picking and pluck-ing at an idea till it came apart at the seams, she hoped they would go downstairs and do it. She wanted to get on with *Peter Pan*. She wanted to see what happened to Peter after the rest of them had gone back home to the Darlings' nur-sery. (*She* wouldn't have left him on his own, like that; she would have insisted he came with them.)

'How does it end?' said Mrs Jenkinson. 'Doesn't it end with Wendy getting married and having a daughter?' She reached out and took the book from Midge. 'Yes, that's right . . . Peter flies off saying he'll come and visit her once a year and take her back with him to do the spring cleaning—'

Mr Jenkinson chuckled. 'A likely tale!'

'She does do the cleaning,' said Midge.

'—then of course she starts to grow up, and, that's it, he loses interest.'

Serve her right for leaving him. Midge wouldn't have.

'In the end he simply stops coming altogether . . simply forgets about her.'

'Finds better things to do,' said Mr Jenkinson.

'Well, that's the point, isn't it? The fact that he's a child and that children are essentially selfish.'

It seemed to Midge, wriggling her toes with ever-increasing impatience, that parents were pretty selfish, going and ruining the ends of books for people. Everyone knew that last chapters were the best, to be read slowly and savoured.

' "And thus it will go on," ' read Mrs Jenkinson, ' "as long as children are gay, and innocent, and heartless." – I don't know that I'd say they were *heart*less, exactly.'

'Of course they are! Hard as nails! And *certainly* not innocent; not these days. I remember, when we were young—'

'Can I have my book back, please?' said Midge.

That night, she dreamt that she was Wendy and went flying with Peter Pan; and when she woke up in the morning the ground was all covered in snow.

4

'That's good!' Mr Jenkinson rubbed his hands together as he gazed out on to the snow-covered ground. 'That's what I like to see! Nice seasonal weather . . . now you'll be able to try out your new sledge.'

Midge knew that what he was really saying was, now *we'll* be able to try out your new sledge. (It had been Mr Jenkinson's idea that a sledge should be one of her Christmas presents. He had been most distressed when they had woken up on Christmas morning to see bright blue skies and not a flake of snow anywhere on the horizon.)

'Where are you going to go? Up Bethany Park? I used to go there when I was a boy. I had this friend called Clive Inkermann. We used to call him Inky . . . Stinky Inky.'

Across the table, unseen by Mr Jenkinson, Sue pulled a face. They heard about Stinky Inky regularly every year whenever there was snow. Mr Jenkinson and Stinky Inky had gone up to Bethany Park together and shot down Bethany Hill on Stinky Inky's sledge so fast that they had ended up buried in a snowdrift. Mr Jenkinson and Stinky Inky . . .

'. . . used to go down there on our bikes, as well. Whoosh! Didn't half shift, I don't mind telling you! One time, I remember—'

'You can get down, Midge, if you've finished,' said Mrs Jenkinson. 'I expect you'll be wanting to get out there before it starts melting.'

'It's not going to melt! Good thick snow, that is. Be here for days. Perhaps this afternoon I'll come up to the Park myself and give it a whirl. How about that?'

Mr Jenkinson looked hopefully at Midge.

'Yes, all right,' said Midge.

'Not this afternoon.' Firmly Mrs Jenkinson reached across for Midge's empty cereal bowl. 'We've got Margaret and Toby coming to discuss arrangements for the march ... just make sure you're back by twelve-thirty, will you, Midge? I want an early lunch.'

Midge fetched her new sledge from the garage. Next door, Damian Gilchrist was industriously shovelling snow away from the garden path. As Midge appeared he looked up, pushed a lock of hair out of his eyes (he had the sort of hair that was very limp and floppy, and the colour of old dish rags) and said, 'Going sledging?'

'Yes,' said Midge. She tugged at the garden gate, the catch of which was a bit stiff, especially with the snow on it. Damian Gilchrist at once threw down his spade and leapt forward.

'Can you manage?'

'Yes, thank you,' said Midge.

She would manage if it killed her. Determinedly, exerting all her strength, she heaved the gate open and dragged the sledge out on to the pavement. It was an extremely good sledge. It had curved wooden runners and was painted bright red.

'For easy spotting in case of snowdrifts,' Mr Jenkinson had said.

She didn't know what Emma would say if they ended up in any snowdrifts. Last year she wouldn't have minded; in fact last year, when they had only had the old plastic dog bed (stolen from Match's dog) they had spent most of their time in snowdrifts. But last year Emma had been quite a different person from how she was now. She hadn't cared so much about her clothes, or getting herself dirty or wet.

Midge trotted on down the road, towing the sledge behind her. She decided that she had better call for Emma first, then they could go on together to collect Match, because Match lived nearer to the Park. Emma lived just a few roads away from Midge in a house that wasn't very big and was always clean and neat. It had neat green shutters at the windows and a wishing well with a gnome in the front garden. Midge had once asked her parents why they couldn't have a wishing well with a gnome. Mr Jenkinson had said, 'What a wonderful idea! I could get some plastic toadstools to go with them,' but he never had.

It was Emma's mother who answered the door. She was very much like Emma, though nowhere near as plump. That was because she lived on a diet of carrot juice (and also because Emma's plumpness was only puppy fat, or so Emma said. People that had puppy fat, according to Emma, almost always grew up thin as rakes.)

'Hallo!' said Mrs Elkins. 'It's Mouse, isn't it?'

'Midge,' said Midge. She hadn't been round to Emma's since before Christmas, but she did think Mrs Elkins might have remembered her name. Not that they had ever gathered at Emma's house as often as at hers or Match's. Mrs Elkins didn't really care for children. She said they cluttered and made mess.

'Midge,' said Mrs Elkins. 'Of course! How silly of me.' She stooped, to straighten up the empty milk bottles on the front step. 'I'm afraid you've just missed Emma. She went rushing straight off after breakfast . . . said something about the snow.'

'Oh.' Midge wrinkled her nose. 'Was she coming round to see me?'

'I don't think so,' said Mrs Elkins.

She could have been, thought Midge. She could have

gone by the passages, and then their paths would have crossed without them ever realizing. Midge would normally have gone by the passages but she hadn't today because of Damian Gilchrist. It would have meant walking right past him. She'd gone the other way, instead, down to the main road.

'I rather think,' said Mrs Elkins, 'that she was going round to see Match – I mean, Antonia. One mustn't call her Match any more, must one? I called her that the other day and was lectured most severely.'

So Match had been round to Emma's. Mrs Elkins even knew that she didn't want to be called Match any more.

'I expect if you hurried,' said Mrs Elkins, 'you might catch her up. She's only been gone a few minutes.'

'Yes,' said Midge. 'All right.'

She turned and dragged the sledge back again, down the Elkins' garden path. It didn't make any sense, Emma going round to Match before coming round to her; not with Match living so much nearer to the Park. It meant they would have to walk all the way back again to collect Midge – because without Midge they wouldn't have any sledge. It was just silly.

The snow was so thick, and so fresh, that she was actually able to follow Emma's footprints. She followed them all the way to the main road, where she temporarily lost them because of there being more people walking to and fro, even early on a Sunday morning, and then picked them up again at the top of Cranley Close, which was where you turned off for Bethany Rise. Bethany Rise was where Match lived, in an old rambly house full of dogs and cats and people. Up and down the path of Match's house, and all round about on the pavement outside, were whole convoys of footprints, but that was not surprising because Match's family were always coming and going, taking dogs out, bringing friends home.

Match's mother came to the door, just as Emma's had done; but unlike Emma's mother she remembered very well who Midge was.

'Hallo, it's the Midget!' she said. She always called Midge the Midget, just as she always called Match the Matchstick. Somehow, with Mrs Gibbs, one didn't mind. 'Don't tell me you've missed them?'

Midge looked at her, forehead crumpled.

'They just went off, about five minutes ago. They had some other girl with them . . . Alison somebody? They said they were going tobogganing.'

Midge's face grew crimson.

'You obviously didn't run into them?' said Mrs Gibbs.

She shook her head; her plaits, under her woolly bobble cap, slapping against her cheeks.

'Well, not to worry, you're bound to find them easily enough, they're only up in the Park . . . I'm sure they'll be happy to see you! All they had was an old tin tray and Robbie's dog bed. That's a very splendid sledge, isn't it?'

It *was* very splendid; but there wasn't much fun having a splendid sledge if you didn't have anyone to sledge on it with. It was ever so mean of Match to go off without her.

'They'll be up on the hill,' said Mrs Gibbs. 'They probably thought you'd go straight there.'

'Yes.' Midge turned, slowly, and began trailing back again down the path.

Mrs Gibbs called after her: 'You'd better hurry, if you want to get some tobogganing in . . . by eleven o'clock that place will be like Brighton Beach!'

Midge put on a little spurt, out of politeness to Mrs Gibbs, but once round the corner, hidden from view, her feet started dragging, making long reluctant scuff marks in the snow. She wasn't sure she wanted to go tobogganing

47

any more. But she couldn't go back home after only twenty minutes. Mrs Jenkinson would be bound to ask awkward questions, like 'Why didn't you stay?' and 'What happened to Match and Emma?'

Mr Jenkinson would be pleased, of course, because it would mean that he could go tobogganing with her instead. But if Mr Jenkinson went tobogganing he would want to go to Bethany Park, because that was where he had gone with Stinky Inky and anyway it was the best place there was, and in Bethany Park they would see Match and Emma, and Match and Emma would see them, and it would be dreadful, to be seen tobogganing with your father while everyone else was doing it with friends. Even Midge knew that she was too old to be doing things with parents.

Maybe Match and Emma *had* expected her to go straight there – maybe they were waiting impatiently for her even now. Suddenly happier, Midge pulled her sledge through the park gates and set off at a jog (as best one *could* jog, ankle-deep in snow) across the tussocky grass and up towards the crest, which ran right along, like a backbone, from one end of the park to the other.

The crest was covered in woodlands, mostly fir trees, looking like Christmas decorations with the snow all sparkly on their branches. Down below was the park, acres of gleaming white, smooth like icing sugar, dotted with tiny bright-coloured figures busily moving to and fro.

The hill – the famous tobogganing hill, down which Mr Jenkinson and Stinky Inky had rushed to their doom – was about a quarter of the way along. Already it was quite crowded. She didn't know whether it was like Brighton Beach, because she had never been to Brighton Beach, but there were four full lanes of traffic on the downward slope – tin trays, wooden sledges, plastic dog beds, milk crates, even old polythene dustbin sacks – and as many going back up.

Midge hauled her sledge to a vantage point and stood, hand shielding her eyes against the dazzle of the sun on her spectacle lenses, searching for Match and Emma. She saw Emma first. She was wearing the new scarlet anorak which she had had for Christmas and she was sitting on an orange-painted sledge just about to take off. Sitting in front of her, on the sledge, was a boy. The boy was Steven Soper and Emma had both arms clasped tight round his middle. As Midge stood watching, the sledge shot forward, down the hill. She heard Emma scream, which was what Emma always did. She had screamed when they went on the Big Dipper at the autumn fair, and she had screamed when they had gone on a day's outing to the sea and the waves had come in and caught her. When Emma screamed it meant that she was enjoying herself.

The orange-painted sledge reached the bottom of the hill and came to a smart full stop. A tin tray and a plastic dog bed, speeding down at the same time, were not so lucky: they ended up by colliding and throwing their passengers out into the snow. One of them was Match. The other two were Alison Soper and an unknown boy. Alison Soper had been on the tin tray: the unknown boy had been sharing Robbie's dog bed.

They were coming back now, up the hill; all five of them in a bunch, laughing, talking, dragging sledges and dog beds. Midge turned and ran, stumbling as she went in the deep snow. She didn't want to be seen by Match and Emma.

Along the crest she floundered, hauling on her sledge. She couldn't go home yet, she hadn't been out nearly long enough. At the far end of the Park, in amongst the fir trees, there was another slope, not really steep enough to be called a hill, and too narrow and hidden away for most people to bother with it. Today there wasn't anyone there at all. Midge set down her sledge at the top of the slope: she would toboggan by herself until it was time to go home.

Dutifully she sat on the sledge and pushed off. Twice she sledged all the way down to the bottom, and twice she toiled all the way back up to the top, but it really wasn't any fun doing it on one's own (especially when only a hundred metres away Match and Emma were doing it with other people and hadn't even bothered calling round to collect her.)

As she stumped her way back up for the second time she became aware of a boy watching her from the top of the slope. He was sitting on the low branch of a fir tree, swinging his legs and obviously waiting for her.

'That your sledge?'

'Yes,' said Midge. What a stupid question, she thought; who else's was it likely to be? She hoped the boy wasn't going to stay there, she didn't like being watched. She always did something silly when people watched her.

Carefully she set the sledge back in position, then bent to take off a gum boot and shake out some snow. Perhaps while she was doing it the boy would go.

The boy did not go. Instead, slithering off his branch he said: 'Can I have a try?'

Midge looked up from her exertions with the gum boot. The boy had come over and was standing beside her. He was a very shabby sort of boy. Everything about him seemed to be ragged. His hair was straggly blond, all wispy and in need of a cut, and his sweater, which might once have been blue, had faded to almost nothing and was so matted and shrunk from being washed that it showed a strip of bare pink flesh round the middle where it didn't reach quite as far as his jeans. The jeans themselves looked

50

like Mr Jenkinson's gardening trousers, being frayed at the edges, with holes in both knees. Also, he was wearing trainers (*trainers* – in the *snow*) and she had a funny kind of feeling, though she didn't like to peer too closely, that he wasn't wearing any socks. His parents must be terribly poor.

'We could get on it together.' The boy gestured at the sledge. 'There's bags of room.'

There *was* bags of room. Midge battled with her conscience as she concentrated on stuffing her foot, in its cosy thick-knit sock, back inside her gum boot. She didn't like boys, in fact she hated them; on the other hand his jeans were all in holes and his sweater was too short and Mrs Jenkinson was for ever lecturing about how people ought to share the good things of life and not just hog them for themselves. She supposed that a new sledge counted as one of the good things.

'It'd go faster with two,' said the boy. 'It'd be more fun.'

'All right.' Midge straightened up. She waved a gloved hand. (The boy wasn't wearing any gloves. No gloves, no socks, you'd think he'd be *freezing*.) 'I'll sit behind, you can sit in front.'

Joyously, he sprang on to the sledge.

'Come on, then! Let's go!'

Midge scrambled on just in time: another second and they were off and away, over the top, going full speed towards the snowdrifts in the valley. The slope seemed steeper than it had before, or perhaps it was just the effect of going faster. The boy kept making loud whooping noises as they went. Once they narrowly missed a tree stump, but he only whooped even louder. Down at the bottom, the drift lay waiting.

'Stop!' yelled Midge; but the boy only whooped.

Headfirst into it they went, just like Mr Jenkinson had

done with Stinky Inky.

'You did that on purpose!' said Midge.

The boy grinned. He had very tiny, sharp white teeth, and his eyes, she noticed, were a brilliant blue (as blue as his sweater had probably once been, before it had had all the colour washed out of it).

'Want to try again?'

'Not if you're going to keep tipping us over!'

He didn't *keep* tipping them over, but he did manage to tip them over more times than he brought them to a proper halt. They were in and out of the snowdrift all morning long. Midge could have taken control of the sledge herself (after all, it was her sledge) but he seemed to enjoy being in command, and pretty soon, in any case, she grew used to ending up in the snowdrift and having to dig herself out and even began to quite enjoy it.

'I wonder what the time is?' she said, as she burrowed out yet again (the snowdrift, by now, was beginning to have the appearance of a rabbit warren). 'I wonder if it's twelve o'clock yet?'

'Dunno.' The boy shook his blond wisps, dislodging the snow. 'Who cares?'

'I do,' said Midge. 'Or at least, my mother does . . . I've got to be back by half past twelve. We've got people coming.' She scrambled up the slope behind him. The seat of his jeans, she couldn't help noticing, was dangerously thin: he would have holes there as well, before very long, if his mother didn't do something. 'I'd better start going back now,' she said.

She held out her hand for the rope of the sledge.

'Not yet!' cried the boy. 'I don't want to go yet!'

'But I must, I promised.'

'So what?' He turned the sledge about-face. 'People are always making promises. No one expects you to *keep* them . . . jump on again, and let's go!'

Four more times they went careering down the slope: four more times they ended up in the snowdrift.

'I really will have to stop now,' said Midge. 'She'll be ever so mad if I'm not there.'

'All right.' Now that he had been allowed to have his own way, the boy accepted it quite cheerfully. 'I'll come with you.'

Midge looked at him, dubious.

'Which way d'you go?'

'Which way d'you?'

'I go over there.' She pointed. There was an exit at the far end which led into Manor Road, which led down to the High Street, which led to Ferris Avenue, which was where the Jenkinsons lived. 'That's the way I go.'

The boy said that that was the way he went, too. Midge wasn't absolutely certain that she believed him, but you couldn't very well stop someone walking with you if that was what they wanted.

They set off together, through the fir trees. Every now and again, as they went, the boy would catch at the branches, bringing down showers of snow upon their heads. Midge didn't mind, because she had her bobble hat.

'You're going to get ever so wet,' she said.

'I like getting wet!' The boy suddenly sprang at a branch, grabbing it with both hands and pulling himself up.

'You'll catch pneumonia if you're not careful,' said Midge.

'What's pneumonia?'

'Something you catch from getting wet.'

'I won't catch it!' Monkeylike, he hung upside down from his branch. 'I never catch things.'

Midge didn't catch things either, as a rule, but she thought that she most probably would if she were only wearing a washed-up sweater and holey jeans. She hauled at the sledge, bumping it along behind her through the trees.

'D'you live near here?'

'Do you?'

'I live in Ferris Avenue,' said Midge.

She waited for the boy to say, 'I live in . . .', but already he had dropped back down to the ground and gone capering off, leaving a powdery trail behind him. He must live up on the Barrow Hill Estate, thought Midge. Barrow Hill was full of poor people, Mrs Jenkinson was always saying it was a crime and a disgrace that human beings should have to live in such conditions. (Emma's mother said it was because they were lazy and stupid and wouldn't work, but that wasn't true because one of the men that came round with the dustcart collecting people's rubbish lived there. He had told Mrs Jenkinson all about it.)

The boy was waiting for her as Midge reached the park exit. He was swinging on the exit gate, to and fro, making runnels in the snow.

'I'm going down there,' said Midge, nodding in the direction of Manor Road.

'So am I,' said the boy. He leapt off the gate. 'I'll race you!'

He reached the end of the road ages before Midge, mostly because of Midge being hampered by the sledge, which kept bumping and banging against her as she ran, but partly because he was wearing trainers. While Midge had to plough, creating deep furrows, he seemed almost to skim the surface, leaving no prints at all.

'Which way d'you go now?' she puffed, as she caught up with him.

'Same way as you.'

Well, you *could* get to Barrow Hill by going up Ferris Avenue. It was a bit of a long way round, but if you didn't have to worry about being back in time for an early lunch because of people coming, then probably it would be a nicer walk than down the High Street with all the traffic.

They turned into Ferris Avenue just as Damian Gilchrist was turning out of it. He beamed soppily at Midge and said: 'Been sledging?' He *knew* she had been sledging. Why did he have to be so stupid all the time? If Midge had been Emma she would have said something smart, like 'No, I've been sunbathing,' but as she wasn't Emma she just nodded and said 'Mm' and went on her way.

'Who was that?' said the boy.

'Soppy idiot that lives next door,' said Midge.

'Don't you like him?'

'No.' Midge heaved, viciously, at the sledge. 'He's *stupid*.'

'Let's chuck a snowball at him!'

Before Midge could say anything (but really, what should she care?) the boy had scooped up a handful of snow and gone skipping back with it down the road. Midge, peering round the corner of someone's garden, saw the snowball hit an unsuspecting Damian *wham*! right in the middle of his back. Damian spun round. If someone had hit Midge in the middle of her back with a snowball she would have been distinctly cross. Damian only looked surprised, and rather hurt. For a moment she almost felt sorry for him, but she couldn't help giggling. Serve him right for being so stupid. At her side, the boy pranced gleefully.

'That was fun! Let's throw some more . . . let's throw one at this silly old bag.'

The silly old bag was Miss Pritchard from over the road. Midge didn't terribly care for Miss Pritchard and Miss Pritchard didn't terribly care for Midge, being the sort of person who thought children should be locked away in cages until they were grown up enough to be what she called civilized. It would certainly serve *her* right to have a snowball thrown at her. On the other hand Miss Pritchard was likely to tell tales, as she had when Midge had broken the head off a sunflower which had been hanging over her garden fence. Vandalism, she had called it, even though it had been the purest accident. Unfortunately, no one could say that throwing a snowball was an accident.

'You better hadn't,' she said to the boy. He had already pawed up a handful of snow and was crouching with it behind a parked car. 'She gets ever so tetchy . . . you'd better not.'

'I want to,' said the boy. He raised his arm, taking careful aim.

'*Don't!*' squawked Midge; but he did.

Miss Pritchard froze in her tracks.

'Flora Jenkinson!' she said. 'How *dare* you?'

'Wasn't me,' said Midge.

The snowball had scored a direct hit: Miss Pritchard's hat was hanging limply off the side of her head. It looked so silly that in spite of everything Midge had a job not to giggle.

'Do not make matters worse', said Miss Pritchard, 'by telling lies.'

'I'm not telling lies!' Midge looked round for the boy, expecting him to own up, as any decent person would. To her annoyance and indignation he was nowhere to be seen.

Miss Pritchard swelled her scanty bosom. (She wasn't *quite* as flat as a pancake, but very nearly.)

'Your behaviour, young lady,' she said, 'leaves a very great deal to be desired. Just don't think you've heard the last of this, because you haven't.'

Miss Pritchard, with her hat still hanging at an angle, tottered on her way up the road. The minute she was out of sight the boy reappeared, bobbing up at Midge's side with a wicked and quite unrepentant grin.

'Got her all right, didn't I?'

Midge looked at him, crossly.

'I told you not to! Now see what you've gone and done. She'll go to my parents, sure as eggs is eggs.'

'Poof!' said the boy, airily.

'It's all right you saying poof, but I'm the one that's going to get into trouble! Why didn't you own up?'

'Why should I?'

''Cos you should!'

'Why?'

''Cos you were the one that did it!'

'So what?'

Midge stared, in outrage.

'You must admit,' said the boy, 'it was jolly funny . . . her going off with her hat all crooked. All tittupy in the snow.'

He minced ahead, being Miss Pritchard all tittupy in the snow.

'That is as may be,' said Midge, in her most severe Miss Jenkinson voice, 'but it's still not fair . . . going and doing something, then not owning up.'

The boy turned, and put his fingers to his nose.

'Don't care!'

'Well, you ought!'

'Well, I don't! So there!'

Midge pursed her lips: there didn't seem to be any answer to that.

They had reached number twenty-six, which was where the Jenkinsons lived. Midge came to a halt.

'This is where I live,' she said, primly. She unlatched the gate. 'I've got to go in now and have my dinner.'

As she pushed at the gate, the front door opened.

'And where have *you* been?' said Mrs Jenkinson. 'Do you realize what the time is? It's getting on for two o'clock! I thought I told you to be back by half-past twelve?'

Midge turned, reproachfully, to look at the boy, but he was no longer there. He must have shot on up the road, past Damian Gilchrist's and along the passages. He was obviously one of those people who took good care to remove himself with all speed at the first sign of trouble.

She supposed it was no more than you could expect from someone who refused to own up when they were guilty.

5

On Sunday evening Miss Pritchard called round to complain; Midge had known that she would. Next morning at breakfast her mother said: 'I do wish you would learn not to be quite such a barbarian. I know she's a bit of an old crotchet, but this kind of thing really doesn't help. We all have to co-exist.'

'And anyway, she's a senior citizen,' said Sue. 'You oughtn't to go round chucking snowballs at senior citizens.'

'I didn't,' said Midge.

Mrs Jenkinson, who had just picked up her newspaper, slowly lowered it again.

'I didn't! It wasn't me!'

'So if it wasn't you, who was it?'

'It was a boy.'

'What boy?'

'A boy that was there.'

'Miss Pritchard didn't say anything about any boy.'

'No, that's 'cos he was hiding behind a car and she didn't see him.'

There was a pause, while everyone looked at her.

'Well!' said Mr Jenkinson. 'That's a new one!'

At school, Lorraine Peters was handing out invitation cards for her birthday party. She had a great stack of them in pretty pink envelopes, decorated with little knots of flowers and people's names neatly printed on the front. Up and down the aisles she marched, chanting as she went: 'CAR-oline, TRA-cey, ALI-son . . .'

Every time she said a name, she dropped an envelope on someone's desk lid. Soon, most of the desks in the room had had a pretty pink envelope dropped on them. Midge didn't like to look too hard, in case people thought that she cared, but she couldn't see another desk anywhere near that was without its envelope, except for hers. Quickly, before anyone could notice, she dumped her school bag on top and began churning about inside it, stirring up the contents so that they were all higgledy-piggledy and out of order, dirty hockey boots on top of clean gym shirt and breaktime bun squashed right down at the bottom.

'What on earth are you doing?' said Emma.

'Looking for something.'

'Well, I can see *that*.'

'So why ask?'

'My!' said Emma. 'Aren't we hoity toity?' She leaned forward to put her face close to Midge's. 'Don't you gnash your little pearls at me!'

It was a horrid kind of day; the kind of day when everyone seemed to be ganged up against her. To begin with, in gym, Miss Southgate announced that instead of having gym they were going to spend the time being weighed and measured, which was quite horrid enough in itself since gym was one of Midge's favourite classes whereas being weighed and measured was just plain boring. Miss Southgate obviously found it pretty boring herself. By the time she got round to Midge she had grown quite irritable and snappish.

'For goodness' sake, child!' She rattled the measuring bar crossly down its pole, ramming it home against

Midge's head. 'When are you ever going to start to grow?'

As if it were *her* fault – as if she were deliberately doing something to *stop* herself growing. She felt disgruntled and hard-done-by, and what didn't help was that everybody laughed.

In Arts & Crafts, which followed, Miss Timbrell said that over the next few weeks they were going to work together to create their own model village, with shops and schools and cottages all made out of paper. She wanted them to think of a suitable name for it.

'Sludgetown,' said Alison, and people started giggling. Miss Timbrell looked faintly annoyed.

'I don't really think Sludgetown is a very suitable name for a model village, do you, Alison? It sounds more like something out of a child's comic to me. Someone else suggest something . . . yes, Flora?'

'Heigh-Ho?' said Midge.

'Heigh-Ho . . . yes, that's good! I rather like that. Hands up for Heigh-Ho Village.'

Midge's was the only hand that went up. Most people groaned, while others made the usual being-sick noises.

'Talk about babyish!' said Lorraine.

In the end they settled for Bedrock St Matthew, after the names of their favourite pop group and its lead singer. Midge thought that was just stupid.

'You could always use Heigh-Ho for your cottage,' said Match, kindly, as they went to break. 'Heigh-Ho Cottage . . . that'd go quite well.'

'Not doing a cottage,' said Midge. 'Doing a church.'

'Oh.' For just a second, Match was obviously at a loss; then she giggled. 'P'raps it could be St Heigh-Ho's?'

'Don't want it to be St Heigh-Ho's.'

It wasn't any use Match trying to be nice. She had been

as mean as could be, going off to the Park like that without her.

'Hey!' Match suddenly poked Midge in the ribs. 'What happened to you yesterday? Someone said they saw you sledging all by yourself.'

'Wasn't all by myself.'

'Oh?' Match seemed puzzled. 'Caroline said you were.'

'Well, I wasn't. I was with someone.'

'Who?' said Match.

'Someone I know.'

Match looked as if she might be going to say something more, but at that moment a shriek came echoing across the playground. The shriek was Emma, going at full tilt along a pathway of ice with her legs splaying out in all directions. Behind her, catching up fast, came Caroline, and behind her, arms waving artistically like something out of Swan Lake, came Lorraine, followed in a bunch by Alison Soper, Judy Marsden and Tracey Nicholls.

'Emma's going to crash,' said Match. Emma did so. 'I knew she would, she can't slide for toffee . . . she fell over *three times* this morning. It's 'cos she lets her legs splay out. I must go and tell her.' Match took a leap forward, across the playground, then stopped. She looked back, uncertain, at Midge. 'You coming?'

Midge shook her head. She wasn't going to go and slide with people who thought she was babyish. And anyway, they didn't want her. *They* had all been invited to Lorraine's party.

Midge walked on, by herself. What did she care? She would go and make a slide of her own; a slide that nobody else knew about. She would play at being IIIB, having a sliding competition. Carlotta would slide the best. She would be graceful, like Lorraine, only more so. She would be like a real prima ballerina. Like a prima *donna* ballerina.

Midge made her slide in a deserted corner of the playing field. The corner was deserted because it was barren and inhospitable, with only a small and scrubby copse of silver birches to give protection from the wind. On the other side of the copse was a farming field, bare and flat and bleak, stretching out into the wide white distance, as far as the eye could see (which in fact was as far as the Barrow Hill Estate). However, it was a good place for sliding.

Midge slid energetically for several minutes. First she slid like Carlotta, prima donna ballerina, with her arms wafting out and one leg stuck up in the air, jumping and turning and doing double-axels, or whatever it was that the ice-skating people did. The judges gave Carlotta nine out of ten. Next she was Tiffany, not quite so flash. Tiffany scored seven. After Tiffany came Samantha, who predictably fell over (though she didn't scream, like Emma). The judges were just about to award Samantha a big *zero*, when from somewhere nearby came the sound of chuckling.

Midge looked up, sharply.

'That was jolly funny!'

From the edge of the copse, the ragged boy was watching her. Midge coloured. (How long had he been there? Had he heard her *talking*?)

'I fell over on purpose.'

'Yes, I know ... you were being someone called Samantha. You said, "Oh for goodness' *sake*, Samantha!" ' The boy bounded forward, on to the slide. 'What's the matter with her? Isn't she any good?'

'She's stupid,' said Midge.

'Like that boy I threw the snowball at. He was stupid.'

'I got into trouble over that,' said Midge. 'You throwing snowballs.'

'Poof!' said the boy.

He glided off down the slide, arms outstretched. He was

wearing the same washed-up jumper and holey jeans as he had worn yesterday.

'How long have you been here?' said Midge.

'Dunno. Can't remember.'

He must have come down from the Estate, ploughing across the fields through the snow.

'Why aren't you at school?'

'Don't go to school. Look!' The boy suddenly kicked his legs away from under him and fell down, laughing, on to his bottom. 'I'm Samantha!'

Midge frowned. 'Everybody has to go to school,' she said. 'I don't.'

She didn't believe him. Of course he had to go to school! He must be playing truant. Lots of the pupils from Barrow Hill did that. Sometimes they were found down the market, helping out on the stalls.

'Now I'm that first one!' The boy floated elegantly, one leg raised behind him in a perfect arabesque. 'What's her name?'

'Carlotta,' said Midge. She had never told the names of her pupils to anyone before. The boy turned at the end of the slide, took a small run and dropped into a squatting position, arms folded across his chest.

'See! Now I'm Carlotta being a Cossack!'

Midge had often wondered whether it would be possible to slide like that. She decided that when she was on her own she would try it.

'What's your name?' she said.

'Haven't got one.'

'Haven't got a name?' She certainly didn't believe *that*. 'You must have. What do your parents call you?'

'Haven't got any parents.'

'You mean you're an orphan?'

'Yes.' He nodded, as he went back again up the slide. 'I'm a norphan.'

Midge wasn't absolutely certain that she believed that, either. And anyway, even orphans had names.

'People have got to call you something,' she said. 'They can't just call you Hey You.'

'Why can't they?'

'Because it would be stupid! And in any case, it wouldn't be allowed ... the Government wouldn't let people go round without having names.'

'So what's yours?'

'Flora Jane Jenkinson,' said Midge.

'That's a name?'

Midge bristled.

'Three names, actually.'

'Three names, *eck*tewlly.' The boy spun on one leg, showing off. 'Fancy! You've got three and I haven't even got one! P'raps I should have one of yours?'

'Don't be silly,' said Midge. 'Mine are for girls.'

'So what's one for boys? What's your *favourite* one?'

'For boys?' Midge wrinkled her nose. Not caring for boys, she hadn't really got a favourite one. Unless, perhaps ... 'Peter?' she said.

'Peter!' The boy clapped his hands, exultantly. 'That's a nice name! That's what I shall be: I shall be Peter. What about you? Who are you going to be?'

'Are we playing a game?' said Midge. Just so long as she knew. 'In that case, if it's a game, I shall be Wendy.' Wendy like in *Peter Pan*. It was a much nicer name than Flora – *certainly* nicer than Midge.

'All right. So I'll be Peter and you can be Wendy. And now that I know where you live, Wendy, I might come and visit you some time. P'raps tonight, if I feel like it. Shall I come tonight?'

'I—' She was on the point of saying that tonight, if he really meant night, and not just after school, wouldn't be convenient since she had her homework to do and anyway

Mrs Jenkinson would never let her go out to play in the dark, specially not with a strange boy, and anyway she didn't know that she wanted him to come and visit her. After all, she didn't like boys. She was just trying to think of a way of telling him so without seeming rude (in case he should think it was because of him being poor and coming from the Estate) when to her horror, pounding down the playing field, passing a hockey ball between them, came Stovey and Marian Cooper. As they drew level, Stovey called out, 'All by yourself, Flora?'

Midge spun round, but the boy had gone. She peered into the copse, expecting him to pop out from behind a silver birch, but there was no sign of him: he had obviously gone running off. Back to school, if he had any sense. Playing truant was just silly, and if ever she saw him again she would tell him so.

She *thought* she saw him again that afternoon, playing by himself on Lorraine and co's deserted slide in the corner of the playground, but it was a long way off and she couldn't be sure. It might have been someone else, like the caretaker's nephew, though the caretaker's nephew didn't normally come into the playground. She was just about to take her glasses off and polish up the lenses with the end of her tie, in the hope of making things a bit clearer, when Miss Alabaster, angrily dotting the blackboard with decimal points, snapped, 'Flora Jenkinson! Pay attention!' By the time she was able to sneak another quick look through the window, the slide was empty and whoever it was had disappeared.

Going home after school she wouldn't have been at all surprised to find a raggedy figure swinging on the school gates or crouched behind a parked car waiting to lob snowballs, but the only peson she encountered was Damian Gilchrist. Damian was in one of his slushy moods, wanting to carry her bag for her even though he had a bag of his

66

own plus his violin case. (Midge thought of the raggedy boy and wondered if he would have wanted to carry her bag. Somehow she didn't think it very likely.)

'I suppose you could always balance it on your head,' she said.

Damian looked at her reproachfully. He was like a big soppy puppy dog. One didn't mind puppy dogs being soppy, they weren't yet old enough to be anything else, but really it was a bit pathetic in a boy of nearly thirteen.

Indoors there was a note from Mrs Jenkinson saying, 'Tea things on table, help yourselves, round at Margaret's, back about eight.' Margaret was one of the CND people. They were planning a special march and Mr and Mrs Jenkinson were on the organizing committee. Mr Jenkinson wasn't terribly keen on organizing but was necessary for driving the car, because Mrs Jenkinson, although quite capable of rebuilding garden sheds when they got accidentally burnt down and able to do even the most complicated of crosswords in about five seconds flat, had a blind spot when it came to machinery and kept failing her driving test on account of reversing up the kerb and crashing into dustbins and not noticing when there was no left-hand turn.

She would probably have failed her cookery test, too, if she had ever had to take one. The Scotch eggs which she had left for tea were more like ancient cannonballs than newly-made Scotch eggs, and the pastry on the gooseberry pie had a distinct look of cardboard.

'Bloody hell!' said Sue, who had arrived indoors just a few seconds after Midge. 'I bet the Russians don't have to put up with this sort of thing.'

Midge, chewing stolidly on a piece of cannonball, was wondering what would happen if the raggedy boy were to turn up as he had threatened. It wasn't the least bit of use him thinking they could go out on the sledge, because it was already dark and she wasn't allowed out in the dark. And she *definitely* wasn't going to ask him indoors. He would just have to go away again. In fact—

'—gone *deaf*, or something?'

Slowly, with puckered brow, Midge looked up.

'Might just as well talk to myself,' said Sue. 'What's the matter with you? What have you gone all broody for? I suppose it's because of your *boy*friend.'

Midge scowled.

'Haven't got a boyfriend.'

'*I* saw you walking down the road with Damian Gilchrist!'

'Damian Gilchrist isn't my boyfriend. I hate him.'

'Why?' said Sue. 'I think he's rather sweet.'

'He isn't sweet, he's yuckish. D'you want some pie?'

'No, I do not, thank you very much.' Sue shuddered. 'Some of us round here care about our figures. Are you going to stay downstairs tonight, or what?'

'Going to do my homework.'

'And play with your dolls? Oh, don't worry!' Sue smiled, sweetly. 'I won't tell.'

Midge didn't have very much homework that night; only a page of maths for Miss Alabaster and that didn't take long because it was percentages and she was good at percentages. She had been thinking of teaching them to IIIB. She opened the wardrobe and began to take them out. Carlotta, Samantha, Louise . . . she wasn't really sure that she wanted to play at being Miss Jenkinson tonight.

Against the windowpane the branches of the old yew tree were tapping. Sometimes pigeons would sit in the yew tree and Midge would open the window for them and entice them in with bits of bread. Maybe there was one there now, wanting shelter from the snow. She walked across, carrying Tamsin, to pull back the curtains and see.

At first, because of the darkness outside and the brightness within, she couldn't make out anything. Then she thought she caught a glimpse of something white, hanging in the branches. She opened the window a crack.

'Hallo, Wendy!' said a voice.

Midge took a startled step backwards.

'Who's that?'

'It's me,' said the voice.

'Peter?' Midge's eyes grew round behind their spectacles. 'What are you doing?'

'I've come to visit you . . . I said I would.'

'But what are you doing in the tree?'

'I like climbing trees.'

'But—' She was beginning to make out the shape of him now, perched like a squirrel amongst the branches. 'Why didn't you come to the front door?'

"Cos I didn't want to.'

'But why—'

'Don't keep asking stupid questions! Open the window, can't you?'

Midge hesitated. Her mother would have a fit if she knew strange boys were clambering in through her bedroom window.

'Look here, Wendy –' his voice was starting to grow querulous '– are you going to let me in or aren't you?'

'Oh, all right,' said Midge. 'But you can't stay.'

'Why not?' Monkeylike, he swung himself into the room. (Midge could hardly bear to watch: it was *so far* to the ground.) 'Why can't I stay?'

'Because you can't! If you wanted to come round you ought to have gone to the front door the same as anyone else.'

Sullenly, he pushed the window shut.

'I don't go to front doors.'

'What d'you mean, you don't go to front doors?'

'I don't go to them!'

'But *why*?'

''Cos they don't like me ... they send me away.'

'Who do?'

'People's mothers.'

Midge fell silent. She could quite see that some mothers might send him away – Emma's mother certainly would. He was looking more shabby than ever tonight. His jumper had a great tear in it and the upper part of his trainers was parting company from the sole. And he still wasn't wearing any socks. She began to think that he really must be an orphan; no proper parents would let their child go round like that. She was just wondering how she could offer him a pair of her own socks without offending him when she became aware that his eyes were fixed on Tamsin, still cradled in her arms. Embarrassed, Midge turned away, flinging Tamsin on to the bed and snatching up *Peter Pan* from her bedside table.

'Look! This is why I said Peter was my favourite name, 'cos this is my favourite book.'

Peter looked, but didn't seem particularly impressed.

'What is it?'

'*Peter Pan*! Have you read it?'

'Can't read.'

Couldn't *read*? Midge had never met anyone who couldn't read. She had been reading almost ever since she could remember.

'Well, don't stand there staring!' He stamped a foot. 'It's very rude to stare!'

Yes, it was; but even so—

'Didn't anyone ever teach you?' she said.

'Don't want to be taught! Let's play something.'

'But how do you manage? If you can't read the names of things? Like roads, and places, and—'

'I manage!' Peter spoke impatiently. 'Stop being boring! I want to play something. Let's play hospitals. I'll be the doctor, you can be a nurse. This can be a bed.' He picked up the little wooden book trough, made by Sue in her woodwork classes, and tipped the books out all over the floor. 'And this can be another. And this.' Rapidly, one by one, he pulled out the drawers in a piece of furniture which had belonged to Midge's grandmother and was known as a nest of drawers. Fortunately, there wasn't very much in them.

'Why should I have to be a nurse?' said Midge, picking up bits of scattered jewellery. 'They're my dolls –' as Peter seized Tamsin and Samantha from the bed and plonked them down on to the hearth rug. '*I* ought to be the doctor.'

'Well, you can't, because I'm going to be.'

'Well, I'm going to be one too, then!'

Peter looked at her, but Midge could be obstinate. It was her bedroom and they were her dolls and what was more he hadn't even been invited. In any case, you couldn't have a doctor that couldn't read. (*That* was what came of playing truant.) She grabbed just in time at Carlotta.

'Don't bash them about like that! If this is a hospital then it means they're ill. They need to be looked after . . . they need bedclothes.'

'Find some!' shouted Peter. 'What's in here?' He pulled open a cupboard door. 'These'll do!'

Between them they made IIIB comfortable in an assortment of sweaters and blouses and thick woolly scarves.

'Now we've got to decide what's wrong with them. *She* could have a broken leg –' Peter pointed at Tiffanny '– and then we could put it in splints. Find something to make splints out of.'

71

Tiffany's splints were made out of Midge's school ruler, broken in two. (It was old, anyway. She had been meaning to buy a new one for ages, one of the see-through plastic sort that you could bend.) Carlotta had a fractured wrist, with her arm heroically done up in a handkerchief sling, while Teresa, suffering from burns, was bandaged all over, top to bottom, like a mummy. Alexandra and Tamsin both had the measles and were covered in spots. Alexandra's spots, having been done by Peter, were all big and blotchy, but Teresa's, done by Midge, were neatly dotted like little pinpoints, because Midge on the whole was a neat sort of person. They were in the middle of an argument as to whether Samantha should have the plague (Peter's idea) or galloping appendicitis (Midge's) when Mrs Jenkinson's voice came up the stairs: 'Midge! We're back!'

'That's my mother,' said Midge.

Peter looked annoyed.

'Already?'

She didn't know why he should say *already* in that cross tone of voice: it was very nearly eight o'clock. They had been bandaging and splinting and painting spots for over an hour. He shouldn't even have been here in the first place.

'Will she come up?'

'I expect so.'

'I'll hide. I'll hide under the bed.'

'I think you ought to go,' said Midge.

'I don't want to go! I like it here.'

'You can't *stay* here.' She didn't care how horrible it was where he lived (and it obviously must be horrible, the way they let him run around all ragged in the snow). You couldn't just march in and take up residence in other people's houses.

'I want to go on playing hospitals. I want to make this one have the plague. I want somebody to die. I want to put

72

them in a coffin. I want to have a burial service and commit them to the earth. I want—'

'Well, you can't!' hissed Midge. 'My mother's coming!'

Mrs Jenkinson's footsteps sounded on the stairs. Peter stood, looking mutinous.

'Midge?' Obedient to the *Private-Keep-Out* and *Trespassers-will-be-Prosecuted* notice, Mrs Jenkinson knocked at the door. 'Is one permitted to enter?'

'Just a minute!'

With one last scorching glare at Peter, Midge stalked across the room. As she reached the door, she turned and looked back. Angrily Peter mouthed, 'Oh, all *right*, if I *must*.'

'So what's happening?' said Mrs Jenkinson. 'Sue said you were doing your homework.'

'Yes.' Midge stood, the door open the merest fraction. 'I've done it.'

'Good! Are you going to come downstairs and have some supper with us?'

'All right, in a minute. I'll just put things away.'

'Well, don't be long, I've got some soup on the go.'

When she went back into the room, the window was open and Peter had gone. She ran across and peered out, into the branches of the yew tree, but he must already have reached ground level and run off. Leaving *her* to clear up the mess. Carlotta in her sling, Teresa in her bandages, Tiffany with her leg all splinted, the others with their spots . . . only Samantha had got away unscathed. Midge picked her up and slung her into the wardrobe. That stupid Samantha! It would be *her*.

6

Next morning, before breakfast, Midge went out into the garden and stood beneath the yew tree. She tilted her head, looking up into its branches. It would be easy enough to climb, if you didn't mind getting scraped, but it was a terribly long way to the top. She didn't think that she would like to try it.

On the walk in to school, which once she had done with Emma but now did alone, because these days Emma preferred to take the bus (it was more grown-up, she said, to take the bus) Midge found herself suddenly attacked by a shower of snow. It wasn't snowballs: it was somebody crouched up a tree, shaking branches.

'*Peter?*' She spluttered snow out of her mouth, brushing it out of her eyes with the back of a gloved hand. 'Is that you?'

He sprang down, laughing, from a small cherry tree. The tree was on the corner of the road where she and Emma had used to meet.

'Gotcha!'

'You just wait,' said Midge.

He danced around her, grinning.

'Betcha can't! Betcha can't get me!'

Midge snatched up a handful of snow from a nearby hedge and hurled it as hard as she could. She hardly saw Peter duck: what she *did* see was the handful of snow hit a passer-by in the middle of the chest. The passer-by was a woman, smartly dressed in furry coat and high-heeled boots. She stopped and glared at Midge.

'Do you mind?'

'Sorry,' said Midge.

The woman stalked on. Peter resumed his dancing.

'Yah! Told you so! C'n I come and play again tonight?'

Midge pursed her lips.

'I don't know. I shall have to ask my mother.'

'It's no use asking *her*! *She* won't let me.'

'She might.'

'She won't! They never do. They hate me.'

Midge looked at him. She wanted to say, 'Perhaps if you were to put some better clothes on . . .' But maybe he didn't *have* any better clothes.

'You can't keep climbing up the yew tree,' she said.

'Why can't I?'

''Cos it's dangerous, and anyway it's not the way people behave.'

'It's the way I behave!'

'Well, it's not the way normal people do.'

'I don't care about normal people! I'm me, I do as I want – and if I want to climb trees I'll climb trees and nobody can stop me, so there!'

'No, but they can stop you coming in through their bedroom windows!'

'If you don't let me in,' said Peter, 'I'll bash and I'll bash until the windowpane breaks!'

'Then you'd get into trouble, 'cos my mother would call the police.'

'Yes, and when they got there I'd have gone!'

'Then I'd tell them where you were . . . I'd tell them you lived on the Estate and that you played truant from school and I'd tell them what you looked like and they'd put out a search warrant and then they'd find you and lock you up.'

Peter's face suddenly crumpled.

'You're just like all of them . . . you hate me!'

Now she felt awful.

'I don't hate you.'

'Then why don't you want me to come and play?'

'It's not that I don't *want* you to—'

'Then why can't I?'

'I didn't say that you couldn't, I—'

'Then I can!'

'I'll have to think about it,' said Midge. Across the street she could see Pearl, in her grey school duffel coat with the hood pulled up. 'I'll have to go now, there's a friend of mine.'

'Where?' Peter spun round, jealously. 'Where's a friend?'

'Over there.'

'That black girl? What's her name?'

'Pearl Chillery.'

'What a stupid name!'

Midge was indignant.

'It's not a stupid name! It's nice.'

'You only say that 'cos she's your friend.'

'No, I don't.' And anyway, Pearl wasn't really her friend; not like Match and Emma had been. They never sat together in class, or did things together out of school. On the other hand, at least Pearl didn't jeer and call her babyish as some of the others did. And Pearl hadn't been invited to Lorraine Peters' party either. That was because she and Lorraine had had a row about some missing gym shoes which Lorraine had accused Pearl of taking. The gym shoes had subsequently turned up in Lost Property, but Lorraine had never apologized. Now she and Pearl weren't on speaking terms.

Midge stepped out on to the zebra crossing.

'Maybe I'll see you later,' she said.

Pearl was standing waiting for her, on the other side of the road.

'Thought you came in with Emma Elkins?'

'Not 'ny more,' said Midge. 'She goes by bus.'

Pearl grunted. She didn't think much of Emma.

'By the way,' said Midge, 'that wasn't my boyfriend just now.'

'What wasn't?'

'That boy I was talking to.'

'Didn't see any boy.' And even if she had, Pearl wasn't interested. She had grievances she wanted to air. 'That Lorraine Peters,' she said. 'She needn't think *I* care. Her and her stupid party. I bet you'll all have to play stupid party games ... *hide* and seek, and hunt the stupid *thimble*.'

As a matter of fact, Midge would have quite liked to play hide and seek and hunt the thimble.

'Just hope you enjoy it,' said Pearl.

Midge frowned. She shifted her school bag from one hand to the other.

'Not going,' she said.

'*You* aren't?' Pearl obviously hadn't realized. 'Why not?'

Midge struggled a moment. 'Wasn't invited.'

Pearl tossed her head: 'I wouldn't go even if I was!'

'No,' said Midge. 'Neither would I.'

'I can't stand her, if you want to know the truth.'

'I can't stand her, either,' said Midge.

'Stuck-up cow.'

She was a bit stuck-up, now one came to think about it. Her and that gang of hers ... Caroline Monahan, Tracey Nicholls, Judy Marsden. They'd always been stuck-up, right from junior school. Just because her aunt was a measly librarian.

'We oughta form a society,' said Pearl. 'The I-Can't-

Stand-Lorraine-Peters Society.'

Midge thought about it.

'We could be the Icastalps.'

'What's that?'

'I-CAn't-STAnd-Lorraine-Peters ... Icastalps.'

'Yeah.' Pearl nodded. 'We could make badges and things.'

'We could find out all the others that can't stand her and we could all wear them.'

'And she wouldn't ever know what it stood for.'

'Not unless we told her.'

'Which we jolly well wouldn't,' said Pearl.

Midge was still thinking about this (after all, if you couldn't stand someone then surely you wanted them to know about it?) when they reached the school gates and found Match and Emma dithering about in a state of agitation.

'Quick!' Match leaped on them. 'Stovey wants you!'

'Wants me?' said Midge.

'Wants *both* of you.'

They looked at each other.

'What for?' said Pearl.

'I don't know!' Match gave a little excited hop. 'That's what you've got to go and find out.'

'What, now?'

'Before assembly?'

'Yes! She said, "I want to see Flora Jenkinson and Pearl Chillery as soon as possible." We've been standing here waiting for you. We thought you'd never come.'

'You'd better get a move on,' said Emma. 'The bell's going to go any minute.'

Pearl stood her ground.

'I haven't done anything wrong.'

'She didn't say you had,' said Match. 'And anyway, she

78

didn't sound mad about anything. More sort of ... *business*like.'

Emma gave Pearl an impatient shove (she was obviously just as anxious as Match to know what it was all about).

'Why don't you just *go?*'

Stovey was waiting for them in the sixth form common room.

'Ah, good!' she said. 'You got the message? I hoped you would. Time is getting short and I need to know what I'm doing ... now, listen! You know the Islip Cup?'

Solemnly, Pearl and Midge moved their heads up and down.

'You know that it's for art? And that art is one of my subjects?'

Again, they nodded. Everybody knew that Stovey was a budding artist: she was going to go to art school in September.

'Well,' said Stovey, looking all keen and eager but in a suppressed sort of way as befitted a member of the sixth, 'Miss Timbrell and I have been discussing it and we're both agreed that I should try going in for it. The reason I've called *you* here is that I can't do it without a bit of help.'

Help? Midge and Pearl glanced nervously at each other out of the corners of their eyes. Stovey surely wasn't suggesting that *they* could be of any use? Neither of them could draw to save their lives, though Pearl had once painted a black cat in the dark which had been quite successful.

'One of the themes for this year,' said Stovey, 'is the multi-racial society, and I've decided—' at this point Stovey grew a bit red and breathless '— I've decided to do something rather special ... rather ambitious. I don't know if it'll work, but anyway I'm going to give it a go. Now, the thing is,' she paused, looking at them, 'I need models. I've already found some – Anna Patel and Jacqui Yoshimura have said they'll sit for me, and I think I can rustle up some more from my brother's school, but I also want some younger people . . . I was wondering if you two would care to oblige?'

They gaped.

'*Us?*' said Pearl.

Us Icastalps? Us nobodies? Anna Patel and Jacqui Yoshimura were both seniors: they were both *some*bodies. Pearl Chillery and Flora Jenkinson weren't anybody at all. (Lorraine Peters could have testified to that.)

'Yes, you!' said Stovey. 'Do close your mouth, Flora, you'll catch a cold standing there with it open like that.' She laughed. 'Honestly! The expressions on your faces! Anyone would think I'd asked you to take part in a bank robbery.'

Or a royal wedding, thought Midge. To be asked to model for one of Stovey's paintings . . .

'You needn't worry I shall want you to pose for hours on end. I work mainly from photographs, so at the most it'll be just one or two camera sessions. How do you feel? Are you willing?'

Willing? Midge swallowed. Pearl, at her side, made a strangled noise.

'Yes?' Stovey beamed. 'That's marvellous! Now I can really get down to it. I thought perhaps if I could just take a few preliminary shots some time with my polaroid . . . are you by any chance free during the lunch hour? Splendid! So how about if we met in one of the art rooms at twelve-thirty? I'll have a word with Miss Timbrell and find out which one we can use. I'll let you know. All right?'

Emma refused to believe it at first, when Midge came back with the news.

'You and Pearl? What's she want you and Pearl for?'

'I can see why she might want Pearl,' said Match. 'I

80

mean, if it's multi-racial.'

There weren't all that many black girls to choose from. But there were hundreds and hundreds of white ones. So why pick on Midge? Stupid, babyish Midge, with her silly little round face and her big pink wally specs. Why not pick on someone pretty, while she was about it? Someone, for instance, such as Emma?

'I can only sup*pose*,' said Emma, after studying Midge for a long while, 'that she's into painting bottled cherries.'

Stovey didn't say anything about bottled cherries when Midge and Pearl went along to the art room (Room 14: all the class had stared when a second-year had put her head round the door with the message) and Midge was too shy to ask. It did bother her, though. Even she was puzzled why anyone should choose to paint her when they could be painting Emma. But as Pearl said, 'Why worry? P'raps she knows we're Icastalps . . . p'raps *she's* an Icastalp. Here, you gonna make some badges for us tonight?'

'Yes, all right,' said Midge. Pearl had managed to discover no less than five other people who declared themselves to be Icastalps. Midge and Pearl had promised to make the necessary badges between them and distribute them first thing tomorrow morning. '*That'll* give her something to think about.'

Midge couldn't help feeling that it would give everyone something to think about (everyone except the Icastalps themselves). She was still pondering the question – because if you had a society for not being able to stand someone, then surely you wanted that someone to know? – when Peter bobbed up at her side. It gave her quite a start, what with her mind being on other things.

'I do wish', she grumbled, 'that you would stop jumping out at people.'

'Why? I like jumping out at people! It's fun.'

'Specially when you give them heart attacks.'

'Poof!' said Peter. He did one of his little twirls. 'Only grown-ups have heart attacks. You're not a grown-up. What time shall I come round to play?'

'I told you,' said Midge. 'I shall have to ask my mother. And anyway, I'm going to be busy tonight.' She had badges to make. 'I'm not going to have time for playing.'

Peter's face slowly crumpled.

'But you said! You said I could!'

'I never,' said Midge. 'I said I'd think about it.'

'You didn't! You said I could! You said I could come and play hospitals! I want to make that girl have the plague. I want to make someone die. I want to have a funeral. I want—'

'I want, I want, I want!' said Midge. It was what her grandmother used to say to her when she was little. 'We can't always do what we want. Sometimes we have to do things that we *don't* want.'

'I don't!' roared Peter. 'I don't *ever!*'

'Then that just means you're spoilt,' said Midge. 'Only people that are spoilt get away with not doing things they don't want. Everybody else is made to.'

'Yah! You're just jealous!'

Midge was outraged: 'I'm not in the least bit jealous!'

'Yes, you are! Jealous as a cat!' He pranced around her, thumbing his nose and chanting in a sing-song: 'Yah-yah, she's jeal-ous, yah-yah, she's jeal-ous!'

'D'you mind me asking', said Midge, in Miss Jenkinson's voice, 'how old you are?'

'As old as I want to be!'

'You act', said Miss Jenkinson, 'as if you're about *five*.'

Peter cackled, and did a somersault in the snow.

'How old are you really?'

'Not telling!'

'Twelve?'

'Might be.'

'Less than twelve?'

He shrugged a shoulder.

'I shall be twelve on April 22nd,' said Midge. 'That makes me a Taurus. What are you?'

'Dunno.'

'When's your birthday?'

'Haven't got one.'

'Oh, don't start *that* again!' Midge stamped a foot. Hadn't got a birthday, didn't go to school . . . '*Every*body has birthdays.'

'Not if they're orphans.'

She was stricken: she'd forgotten about him being an orphan.

'You mean you really and *truly* don't have birthdays? Nobody ever sends you cards or gives you presents?'

'What's presents?'

'Presents! For your birthday. Like last year, when I was eleven, I had a bicycle.'

Peter's eyes grew big.

'You've got a *bi*cycle? Would someone give me a bicycle if I had a birthday?'

'Well . . . they might do,' said Midge.

'Would you give me one? If I had a birthday?'

'I'd give you a present,' said Midge. 'I couldn't actually afford a bicycle, but—'

'What could you afford?'

'I could afford . . .' she was about to say, a book, but then she remembered: he couldn't read. 'I could afford to buy some wool and knit you a scarf. I'm good at knitting. I could do a great long one, all in stripes, and I could—'

'I don't want a scarf! Scarves are soppy!'

'Oh. Well—' Midge tried hard not to be offended. After all, it wasn't his fault if he were an orphan and had never had any birthday presents or been taught any manners.

83

'*You* choose something – only it'll have to be something small, 'cos I haven't really got much money. You say what you'd like, and I'll say if I can afford it.'

'I'd like a gun.'

'A *gun*?' Midge's face fell. 'I couldn't buy you a gun!'

'Why not? Guns don't cost much.'

'No, but they're dangerous.' Mrs Jenkinson hadn't ever let Midge or Sue have guns to play with.

'I'd only want a *pretend* one.'

Midge was silent.

'If I had a gun I could be a gunman, or a hijacker, or a great train robber.'

'They're all *bad* things,' said Midge.

'But they're fun!'

'Not if they go round shooting people. Why can't you have something like . . .' She racked her brains trying to think of the sort of thing which might appeal. She didn't really know what boys enjoyed doing, apart from fighting and playing football. '. . . a football,' she said.

'I don't want a football! I want a gun! It's not fair! You say that I can choose and then when I do you tell me I can't have it!'

Midge bit her lip. He was quite right: it *wasn't* fair. Especially when it was the first birthday present he'd ever had.

'P'raps it could be just a very *little* gun,' she said.

'So long as it looks like a real one.'

She wasn't at all sure that she knew what a real gun looked like. Peter leapt up, joyously, pretending to shoot into the air. He was happy, now that he had got his own way.

'When can I have it?'

'Well, if it's a birthday present,' said Midge, 'you oughtn't really to have it till it's your birthday.'

'So when is it my birthday? Is it today?'

'Saturday,' said Midge.

'Saturday's days away! I can't wait till Saturday! I want it now! I want to play with it, I want—'

'Stop saying *I want* all the time! It's very bad manners, and it's childish.'

Peter looked sullen.

'So what?' He kicked at a pile of snow with his tattered trainers.

'So I won't give you a present at all,' said Miss Jenkinson, 'if you're not more polite.'

'But if I'm p'lite you'll give it me on Saturday?'

'Yes. If you are.'

'I will be! I will be! Look.' He suddenly fell to one knee in the snow. 'Here I am, being it . . . dear Wendy! If you give me my present on Saturday I shall love you for ever and ever and say all nice things to you, like you're the most beautifullest prettiest nicest kindest girl that ever lived, and maybe, if you wish, I shall even give you a kiss . . . there!' He leapt to his feet again. 'That was p'lite enough, wasn't it?'

Midge had to agree that it was (though she was rather alarmed at the prospect of being kissed).

'In that case, I'll go now.' He sprang off, down the road. 'You will make sure that it looks *real*, won't you?'

He had obviously forgotten about wanting to come round and play hospitals. It was really just as well. She had quite enough to do, making badges for the Icastalps and writing essays for Miss Kershaw; and anyway he might have blurted out about the gun, and *then* there would be trouble.

7

The other members of the Icastalps were Trisha Walters, Diane Whalley, Susan Sloman, Susan Openshaw and Jennifer Goodchild. Midge and Pearl handed out their badges first thing before Assembly, and they all trooped into the assembly hall wearing them. Throughout prayers and hymn singing people kept pointing and raising their eyebrows, and afterwards, in the classroom, they found themselves subjected to a barrage – 'What is it? What's it stand for? Tell us!' – but Pearl had sworn them all to silence.

'Just have to guess, won't you?' said Trisha.

Lots of people tried, but no one came anywhere near. Most people got stuck after the first three or four letters, though Lorraine Peters, of all people, came up with International Conspiracy against St Anne's Loopy Perverts (St Anne's being a Catholic school on the other side of town, against whom they quite often played netball and hockey matches). Even Pearl had to admit that it was a good try.

'Nowhere near the truth, of course . . . she won't ever guess the truth.'

'Why don't we *tell?*' urged Trisha. Like Midge, the others couldn't altogether see the point of having a secret hate society. They weren't quite sure what purpose it served. Pearl, however, only tossed her plaits and said: 'Tell? I'm not gonna tell her!' And if Pearl wasn't going to tell, then

86

nor must any of the others. It was understood that there would be Trouble If They Did. It was hard to escape the conclusion that Pearl, rather like Lorraine herself, had just the tiniest tendency towards *bossiness*.

That lunch time there was an Under-13s hockey practice. As they changed together in the cloakroom, Match said: 'What *is* this Icaslap thing?'

'Icastalp.'

'Icastalp . . . what is it?'

'I can't tell you.'

'Why not?'

''Cos it's a secret.'

Match looked at her, reproachfully. There had once been a time, and not very long ago, when the three Ms would never have dreamt of having secrets from one another.

'I wouldn't tell anybody,' said Match. 'Honest.'

Midge knew that she wouldn't. Emma might have done, but not Match; not if she had given her word. For just a moment, old loyalties wrestled with new: Match and the three Ms against Pearl and the Icastalps. The trouble was, the three Ms no longer existed. Emma had told her that, and Match had not disagreed.

'I can't,' said Midge. 'I promised.'

Match didn't say any more, but Midge knew that she was hurt.

For the next two days the Icastalps went round in a bunch, enjoying their new-found popularity. On Thursday a message came through that Stovey would like to see Pearl and Flora in the sixth form common room to arrange for a proper camera sitting. When they came back with the news that they had actually been asked round to Stovey's house on Sunday morning ('for coffee and biscuits as *well*') the popularity of the Icastalps knew no bounds.

The very next day, Lorraine came up to Midge and with the air of a conspirator pushed a pink envelope into her hand.

'This is for you,' she said.

Midge looked at it.

'It's an invitation to my party . . . I'm ever so sorry I didn't invite you before. I meant to – I thought I *had*. You were on the list.'

Midge took the invitation card out of its envelope. *Ms Lorraine Peters*, it said, *requests the pleasure of Ms Midge Jenkinson's company at her birthday party to be held on Saturday 22 February at 14 Verdayne Gardens from 2.30 p.m. to 6.00 p.m. RSVP.*

'You don't have to RSVP if you tell me now,' said Lorraine. 'My mother said she'd like to know immediately because of getting things in.'

Because Saturday 22 February was tomorrow, which didn't give Mrs Peters very much time.

Midge looked down at her invitation card.

'Have you invited the others?' she said.

'What others?'

'Trisha, and Tracey, and—'

'Oh! That lot.' Lorraine spoke scornfully. 'No, just you and Pearl. I wouldn't invite *them*.'

But they were Icastalps, and Icastalps had to stick together. They had to, because they had made a pact – and anyway, Midge and Pearl had both sworn that *they* wouldn't go to Lorraine Peters' party even if they *were* invited.

'I really thought I'd given you a card,' said Lorraine. 'I don't know how I could've missed you . . . I must have ticked you off by mistake. You will be able to come, won't you?'

Midge drew a breath.

'I'd like to,' she said (it was true: she *would* have liked to), 'but I'm afraid I'm doing something else on Saturday. If you'd asked me last week—'

'I'm ever so sorry,' said Lorraine. 'I really thought I had.'

At breaktime, before the Icastalps could gather in that part of the playground which had recently become their patch, Pearl jerked her head at Midge as a sign that she wanted to speak to her.

'Is it about Lorraine?' said Midge.

'Sh!' Pearl put a finger to her lips. 'Downstairs.'

She led the way down to the cloakrooms and they crammed together in one of the lavatories, which was where first years usually crammed themselves when they wanted to be private. (Second years, being a bit more sophisticated, tended to gather in the games cupboard beneath the back stairs.) There in the gloom, with the door fast shut, they waited, listening until the sounds outside had died away; then:

'What are we gonna do about the Icastalps?' said Pearl.

'What d'you mean, what are we going to do?'

'Well, now that she's come round.'

'Come *round?*'

'Invited us to her party!'

Midge, with her back pressed to the door, stared at Pearl, unconcernedly sitting on the lavatory seat.

'You didn't say you'd *go!*'

'Why, didn't you?'

Midge's face grew crimson.

'You said you wouldn't!'

'Yeah, but that was before.'

'Before what?'

'Before she apologized – about the gym shoes. You know? She actually apologized.'

'She only did it 'cos of Stovey! 'Cos we're going to be in her painting.'

'Yeah, but you can't bear a grudge for ever, can you? Not when someone's actually apologized. If she hadn't've apologized I'd have told her to get knotted.'

But as it was, she had said that she would go to the party. And when you went to someone's party you couldn't very well walk around with a badge saying you couldn't stand them; even Midge could see that.

'So I dunno what you're gonna do,' said Pearl. 'Whether you're gonna go on being an Icastalp, or—'

'Doesn't seem much point any more,' said Midge.

There never had really been much point, except that it had been her and Pearl. The other Icastalps were just dregs. They probably couldn't help being dregs, but that was what they were, and some of them actually could help it. Jennifer Goodchild could. She didn't *have* to be greedier than a pig, any more than Susan Openshaw had to keep boasting about the swimming pool in her back garden. Any more than Trisha had to be so stupid all the time and Diane Whalley pick her nose and keep eating it. Diane Whalley was disgusting. So was Susan Sloman, with wax all coming out of her ears. It wasn't any wonder Lorraine hadn't wanted to invite them to her party.

At lunch time, when the Icastalps (what was left of them) went to huddle on their patch, Midge didn't go and huddle with them. She didn't feel like watching Diane pick her nose or hearing Susan Openshaw going on about her swimming pool, or the others repeating in chorus how they couldn't stand Lorraine Peters.

'Conceited cow!'

'Stuck up so-and-so!'

'Who's she think she is, anyway?'

It probably wasn't fair, when she had been one of the founder members, but Midge just couldn't get that interested in hating Lorraine any more.

For want of anywhere better to go she wandered over

the playing field to look at her slide, but the weather had turned warmer and the slide was starting to melt. She prodded at it disconsolately with the toe of her shoe.

'It isn't any good,' said a familiar voice. 'I already tried it.'

Midge jumped, crossly.

'You're doing it again!'

'Doing what?'

'Springing out on people!'

'I didn't spring out, I've been here all the time.' Peter sounded aggrieved. 'I've been waiting for you . . . I waited for you yesterday, *and* the day before. Why didn't you come?'

''Cos I had things to do.'

'What things?'

'If you must know,' said Midge, 'I've been playing hockey – and anyway, you oughtn't to be here. You're trespassing. This is private property.'

'Why? Who's it belong to?'

'It belongs to my school, and if anyone finds you you'll get into trouble.'

Peter didn't say 'Poof!' as he usually did. Instead he backed into the copse, amongst the silver birches, and beckoned to Midge to follow him.

'Come and hide!'

'*I* don't have to hide,' said Midge. 'I'm allowed here.' But she went, all the same. Even talking to Peter was better than not talking to anyone.

'Did you get my gun?' he said.

She had forgotten all about the gun.

'No, I didn't . . . I told you, Saturday.'

'Isn't today Saturday?'

'Of course it isn't!' If he didn't keep playing truant from school he would know perfectly well that it wasn't.

'So when will it be?'

91

'Tomorrow,' said Midge.

'So tomorrow you'll have my gun?'

'Ye-e-es.' She said it reluctantly. 'I s'pose so.'

'You promised! You promised! You can't not get it now!'

'I'll *get* it,' said Midge. Really, she thought, she had never known anyone so childish. But then, if he hadn't any parents and never went to school . . .

'When will you give it me?'

She considered the matter. 'After lunch.'

'When's after lunch?'

'Half past two.' Half past two, when Lorraine's party was due to begin. 'I'll meet you in the passage that runs along the bottom of our garden. There's a gate there. It's painted green, and it's got the number ten printed on it, so you'll know which one it is.' If he could read numbers. She looked at him, doubtfully: he was such a very *ignorant* boy. 'Like this . . . one-o.' She wrote it in the snow with the tip of her shoe. 'Right?'

'Right.' He nodded. 'One-o.'

'At half past two.'

'At half past two,' said Peter. 'I'll remember.'

On Saturday morning, Midge raided her money box pig. The pig had a slit in the top for putting money in, but no way of getting it out again unless she lay flat on her back on the floor, poking about with a nail file. It was a slow and bothersome business, and furthermore it made one's arms ache. Midge had to keep reminding herself that she was doing it in a good cause, though she had doubts even now as to whether buying someone a gun really *was* a good cause. She knew her mother wouldn't think so. But then Peter was a boy, and boys always had guns, or weapons of some kind. In books they did. If it wasn't guns it was catapults or bows and arrows. Peter in *Peter Pan* had had a sword, and what was more it had been a real one. At least the gun would only be pretend.

After lunch, with her purse bulging with coins and safely tucked away in the pocket of her duffel coat, Midge set off into town. There was a big toy shop in town called Hussey's, which had the toys all laid out like goods in a supermarket, so that you could just pick up what you wanted and take it in a wire basket to the check-out. It would be easier, she thought, than having to go up to an assistant and ask. In fact she wasn't at all sure that she would be brave enough to do that; not even for Peter, even though she had promised.

There were lots of guns in Hussey's. Big black ugly ones that looked almost real, elegant silvery ones with revolving chambers, thin spindly ones nearly as tall as Midge herself, short stubby ones that turned out to be water pistols, and all manner of shapes and sizes in between. The silvery ones were the prettiest, but they were too expensive. The water pistols were the cheapest, but maybe a water pistol wasn't the same as a gun, and then Peter would be disappointed and would get cross.

In the end, after glancing guiltily over her shoulder in case anyone should be watching, Midge picked a little red gun and walked with it to the check-out. Her throat had gone all dry. She really thought, when the girl at the till leaned forward, that it was to press a secret switch that would ring a secret bell that would bring a store detective out to arrest her, but nothing happened. The gun was wrapped up and Midge walked out with it in her pocket just the same as if it had been a book or a box of crayons (though she still half expected someone to come running after her).

It was only a quarter past two when she arrived back

home but Peter was already there, waiting where she had told him to wait, in the passage that ran past the bottom of the garden.

'Did you get it?' he cried.

'Yes, but I haven't had time to do it up or buy a card or anything.'

'That doesn't matter!' Peter was jumping up and down in excitement. 'Where is it? I want it! Give it to me!'

He really ought to be made to say please, thought Midge; but perhaps she would let him off just this once, seeing as it was the very first birthday present he had ever had.

He snatched the gun from her, tearing it out of its wrapping and letting the empty box and the paper fall to the ground. Midge, pursing her lips (hadn't anybody ever taught him *any*thing?) bent to pick it up.

'Bang-bang!' yelled Peter, pointing at her with his gun. 'You're dead!'

'Don't shout,' said Midge, nervously. The last thing she wanted was either of her parents coming out to investigate. 'And don't point it at people.'

'Silly old fusspot!' Peter turned, smartly, on an unseen enemy, clutching the gun with both hands. 'Take that, you scum!'

Midge watched him a moment.

'You haven't said thank you,' she said.

'Thank you!' Peter stuck the gun up into the air. 'Enemy aircraft ... this is a machine gun ... rat-a-tat-a-tat-a-tat!'

'Do you like it?' said Midge.

'It's all right. It's a bit small – and the colour's all wrong. You don't have red guns. Why didn't you get a black one? I'd have rather have had a black one.'

He had obviously forgotten that he was going to tell her she was the nicest, kindest, most beautifullest girl in the

94

world. She could have reminded him, but then he might have remembered that he was going to kiss her, and she really didn't think that she wanted to be kissed.

'Let's play something!' Peter stuck the gun in the waistband of his jeans. 'Let's play bank robbers . . . I'll be the robber and you can be the lady behind the till, and then when I've got the money and I'm making off in my getaway car you can be a p'licewoman coming after me.'

'All right,' said Midge. 'But we'd better go to the far end of the passage and do it.'

She was a bit dubious, at first, about playing bank robbers. It wasn't at all like the games she normally played. She didn't quite know what she was supposed to, and whatever it was she felt fairly certain that she oughtn't to be doing it, though after all it was only make-believe and it wasn't as if she were the one who was being the robber or carrying the gun, indeed *she* was the one who was trying to catch the robber and stop him carrying the gun, so perhaps it really wasn't as bad as all that. Even Mrs Jenkinson could hardly object to people trying to stop people shooting people.

'Now you're the p'licewoman,' shrieked Peter, 'coming after me!'

Away down the passage they screamed, Peter in his getaway car, brakes squealing, tyres screeching, gun still blasting, Policewoman Jenkinson hot on his heels. Down the passage, round the corner, into Ferris Avenue, up past number ten, back into the passage . . . playing at bank robbers was really quite fun.

'Eeee-aaa, eeee-aaa, eeee-aaa,' wailed Midge, being a siren.

Peter came to a stop.

'I've had enough of this one! I've got away with the money, let's play something else now. Let's play terrorists planting bombs. I'll be the terrorist, you can be a woman from MI5 that's after me. You can have the gun, if you like.'

Midge recoiled.

'I don't want the gun!'

'You've got to, if you're MI5. They always have them. They couldn't catch people otherwise.'

'But what'll you have?'

'I'll have my bomb.' Peter made a sudden dart at the wall which lined one side of the passage. The wall was old and crumbly. 'Look!' He lifted half a brick off the top. 'This is my bomb that I'm going to plant . . . I'm going to plant it somewhere along here and you've got to try and stop me. We'll walk halfway down . . . 'bout *here*. Now you close your eyes and count up to twenty-five and when you've got to twenty-five you can come after me, but not before.'

'All right.' Obediently, Midge closed her eyes. 'I'm going to start counting *now* . . . onetwothreefour—'

'An' no cheating!'

She was too busy counting to retaliate.

'—twenty-one, twenty-two, twenty-three, twenty-four, twenty-*five!*'

Midge opened her eyes and tore off along the passage. With any luck, if she'd taken the opposite route to Peter, she'd bump into him on his way round.

She didn't bump into Peter, she bumped into Miss Pritchard. Miss Pritchard gasped and said, 'Really!'

Midge ran on. She couldn't stop, she had a terrorist to catch. She could see the terrorist, just turning into the passage ahead. He had taken the same route as her. Dimly, as she redoubled her efforts, she heard Miss Pritchard's voice: '. . . tell your mother about you!'

Midge screeched into the passage just in time to catch Peter lobbing something over the back gate of number ten. He was actually daring to plant his rotten bomb in the garden of her own house! Midge dropped to one knee with her gun, as she had sometimes seen people on the television do (on those rare occasions when Mrs Jenkinson hadn't come rushing in to turn it off).

'Freeze,' she yelled, 'or you're dead!'

Peter froze – and so did Midge. For at that precise moment, her mother's head appeared over the gate.

'*Midge!*' Her voice was full of outrage. 'What on *earth* do you think you're doing?'

8

'Please may I get down now?' said Midge.

'Of course you may, if you've finished.'

'I have finished.'

'Very well, then, off you go! See you at lunch time.'

'Going round to the great Stovey's, are we?' Mr Jenkinson looked up and winked. For some reason, he always seemed to find the name Stovey amusing. 'And where does the great Stovey hang out?'

'Firsby Avenue.'

'Firsby Avenue, eh? So how are you getting there? Bike?' Midge nodded. 'Well, watch how you go.'

'And if you find any more guns,' said Mrs Jenkinson, 'just leave them where they are. I don't want a repetition of yesterday.'

Yesterday Mrs Jenkinson had been crosser, almost, than Midge could ever remember. It hadn't just been the gun, but the brick thrown over the garden wall. Peter, of course, had done one of his disappearing acts, taking to his heels and streaking off up the passage so fast she had scarcely even seen him go. Midge had been left, the sole culprit. (The gun had been broken up and thrown into the dustbin.)

'You want to stick to your dollies,' said Sue, as Midge got down from table. 'Much nicer for little girls than guns.'

'Much nicer for anybody than guns!' snapped Mrs Jenkinson.

Firsby Avenue, where Stovey lived, was partly big old houses, hidden from the road behind yew trees and holly bushes in dark, dampish-looking gardens, and partly blocks of modern flats. Midge was glad when Stovey's turned out to be one of the big old houses. She liked old houses.

She wheeled her bicycle up the crunchy path (taking care to shut the gate behind her, which Mrs Jenkinson said you should always do in case of small children or dogs: she bet Peter never bothered) and was just wondering where she should leave it when the front door opened and Stovey appeared.

'Hallo!' she said. 'You're nice and early. Dump your bike in the porch and come on up to the studio. Pearl's just this minute got here as well.'

Stovey was wearing blue jeans and an old holey sweater with the sleeves rolled up. It wasn't quite as holey as Peter's, but it was certainly old. *And* it was painty. Midge began to wish that she had also put on a sweater and jeans. Her mother had said she ought to wear something decent if she were going to be photographed. She had suggested 'that nice tartan dress we got you for Emma's party last year.' The tartan dress felt a bit silly now, as she followed Stovey's blue-denimed legs up the stairs, but then they reached the studio, a long, tall room just beneath the roof, and there was Pearl all demure in red velvet with a white lace collar, looking quite unlike her normal self, and of course it was quite true, they *were* going to be photographed and one ought to dress up a bit for a photograph. Stovey wouldn't want a couple of gutter urchins in her painting.

'We'll concentrate on business first,' she said, 'then when that's out of the way we can chat.'

Chat! How Match would grow pink if she knew.

For almost an hour Stovey took photographs of the two of them. First she took some more polaroids, and then she

99

took some proper ones using a real professional camera with a flash, which she said belonged to her father.

'He's a photographer with the local paper. He does portraits as well – don't screw your face up like that, Flora! It makes you look like a gargoyle – so if ever you want any pretty pictures of yourselves – smile, Pearl! – you know where to come. In fact – *smile!* – if these are any good I'll run you off some prints. Right, let's try some from a different angle. Do you think, Flora, that you could go and perch on that stepladder over there? Right up at the top . . . then we'll have Pearl just beneath you . . . yes! Like that! That's fine. Hold it, now.'

When she had taken all the photographs she needed Stovey plugged in an electric kettle which stood on a table in the corner, together with some mugs and a carton of milk and some interesting-looking cakes in all different colours, and said that while they were waiting for the water to boil she would show them her sketch for the painting.

'This is it, you see.' She jerked at a piece of old dirty sheet which Midge had noticed hanging about but had been too polite to look at in case it was a sheet for sleeping on, which would have been rather dreadful, the state it was in. Obviously it *had* been a sheet for sleeping on but had now become a sheet for covering up paintings, for underneath it, propped against an easel, was Stovey's sketch. Midge and Pearl stood reverently, lost in admiration and wondering what to say.

'It's big,' said Pearl, 'in't it?'

'It is big,' agreed Stovey. 'That's why I needed so many models . . . I told you it was ambitious! What does it remind you of? Does it remind you of anything?'

'Kind of like—' Pearl scratched her ear.

'Like a nativity?' said Midge, shyly.

'Yes!' Stovey beamed. 'That's exactly what it is! In the style of the old masters, but modern, you see . . . all the different nationalities. Here's Anna – and this is Jacqui. These are two of my brother's friends. Shall I show you where you're going? Up here, look.' She tapped a finger on the top left-hand corner of the paper. 'You're going to be a pair of little angels . . . do you think you'll like that?'

Pearl giggled. 'My mum will!'

'Why? She thinks you're angelic, does she?'

Pearl giggled even more.

'How about you, Flora? You don't look too sure. What's the problem? Don't you fancy the idea of being an angel?'

Midge chewed at a piece of fingernail.

'Do angels look like bottled cherries?'

'Do angels look like *what?*'

'Bottled cherries.'

'Bottled *cherries?*'

Cheeks scarlet, Midge mumbled, 'Someone said it was what you said I looked like.'

'I said you looked like a bottled cherry?' Stovey's face suddenly cleared. '*Botticelli!*'

There was a pause.

'What's a bottychelly?' said Midge.

'Botticelli – the painter! Haven't you ever heard of him? Good heavens! I thought everybody had heard of Botticelli. In fact what I actually said, because I remember it now very well, it was that day you were playing hockey, what I actually said was that you looked like a little Botticelli angel. If I had a picture I'd show you one . . . they're very attractive, you know, Botticelli angels.' Stovey went across to the table to turn off the kettle. 'Maybe I should take you both up to London sometime, to the National Gallery? Then you could see for yourselves. Coffee or chocolate, by the way? The chocolate's nicer. We could even go there tomorrow, if you wanted. If you're not doing anything else, that is.'

Tomorrow was half term. Midge wasn't doing anything at all. Neither, it seemed, from the way she gaped, was Pearl.

'Shall we do that?' said Stovey. 'Would you like to?'

Midge and Pearl, big-eyed, made scraping noises in the backs of the throats. (THEM – going up to town with Stovey!) Stovey laughed.

'Now you look more like a couple of goons . . . standing there with your mouths gaping open! Do you want to see your photographs?' She handed them the polaroids which she had taken. 'You can have them, if you like, when I've finished with them, though they do rather tend to fade . . . look at this one, Flora, where we tied your plaits up. I like that one! Have you ever thought of having your hair cut short? It would really suit you. You've got such a nice little round face . . . I shall paint you with short hair. I'm going to do Pearl with all her plaits. That'll give me something to work on! Here, help yourself to cakes. They're a bit lurid, I'm afraid, but you can blame my mother for that . . . she thinks it's the sort of thing that first years like.'

It *was* the sort of thing that first years liked. Midge and Pearl sat happily munching, clutching their mugs of hot chocolate.

'You know, you are most awfully lucky, you two,' said Stovey. 'You've both got such unusual names . . . Pearl and Flora. Lovely!'

Pearl promptly made a being-sick noise: Midge wrinkled her nose.

'Don't you like them?' said Stovey, surprised. 'I suppose nobody ever does like their own name. When I was your age, I remember, I most desperately wanted to be called Polyanthus . . . Polyanthus Stovewell! Can you imagine?'

'I'd like to be Rita,' said Pearl.

'Rita? Oh, no! That's horrible. Almost as bad as Polyanthus. Pearl's such a pretty name; so is Flora.'

They looked at her, doubtfully.

'Pearl's lovely and soft-sounding – and of course Flora's so romantic!'

'Romantic?' said Midge.

'Yes ... Flora Macdonald and Bonnie Prince Charlie!'

Midge considered it: she'd never thought of Flora in connection with Bonnie Prince Charlie.

'The Skye Boat Song,' urged Stovey.

'Yes ...' she thought about the Skye Boat Song. It was quite a nice sort of song, but Flora still sounded like a grandmother name. 'I'd rather be called Wendy,' she said.

'Oh, not Wendy! Surely? That's terribly twee. It makes me think of that awful girl in *Peter Pan*, always mothering people and tidying up after them and cooking their meals.'

'But it was in the reign of Edward VII,' said Midge. 'Girls were different then.'

'Yes; I suppose so.' Stovey bit into a cake and regarded it thoughtfully. 'Of course, you were reading *Peter Pan*, weren't you? Did you like it? I did when I was young, but I don't know if I would now ... I used to think Peter was rather bold and dashing. But I think if one actually knew anyone like that he would be a frightful bore ... never growing up, and everything. Boys are really quite impossible at that age, aren't they? Don't you find them so? I always think girls mature so much quicker. Have another cake each – if you don't eat them up they'll only go to waste. And look, before you leave, let's arrange about tomorrow. What time shall we meet? Ten o'clock, at the station? Just check with your mothers that it's OK. Tell them the treat's on me, so you won't have to worry about train fares or anything ... it'll be my thank you to you both for coming and sitting for me.'

Midge rode home, face glowing, on her bicycle. Just wait

till she told Match! Just wait till she told *Emma*.

'Stovey said I was like a little Bottlejerry angel. Stovey said I had a nice little round face. Stovey said—'

'Hands up or I'll shoot!'

Midge wobbled and almost fell off. She skidded to a halt, one foot on the ground.

'If you do that just once more I'll murder you!'

Peter emerged, grinning, from behind a pillar box.

'Did I frighten you?'

'It's not funny,' said Midge. 'It's just *stupid*.'

The grin left his face. He kicked sullenly at an empty Coca Cola can in the gutter.

'What are you all dressed up for?'

''Cos I've been to have my photograph taken.'

'What for?'

''Cos I'm going to be in a picture.'

'What sort of picture?'

'A picture that's being painted by one of the prefects at my school. It's for a competition. And if it wins –' Midge paused, self-important, '– it'll go on exhibition all over the country.'

Peter kicked again at his empty Coca Cola can. He didn't seem too impressed.

'I've just been round there,' said Midge, carelessly. 'Just for a chat and to look at my photographs. Stovey says I can have them when she's finished.'

Peter looked at her, jealously.

'Who's Stovey?'

'She's the one that's doing the painting.'

'Is she that girl that spoke to you that time? That big girl with the hockey stick?'

'Yes. She's really nice.' Midge was beginning to feel that perhaps she, too, might be starting to have a thing about Stovey. 'She's going to take us up to London tomorrow . . . to the National Gallery. We're all meeting at the station at ten o'clock and she's going to treat us and pay our fares. She's going to show us some Bottle . . .' Midge hesitated. '. . . Bottlejerries. 'Cos that's what she says I look like, like a Bottlejerry angel. Course, I don't s'pose *you* know who Bottlejerry is.'

'Don't want to know!' Peter aimed a swipe at someone's hedge. 'Where's my gun?'

'She broke it up,' said Midge. 'She threw it in the dustbin.'

Peter turned crimson. 'Broke up my gun?'

'Yes.' Midge was tempted to add, and serve you right, but thought that maybe it mightn't be quite fair. It had really been her fault more than his. She had known all along she oughtn't to be playing at bank robbers with him. 'She was ever so mad at me. She went on and on. That brick you threw landed on one of her glass things that she grows plants in.'

Peter didn't care about the glass thing.

'I want my gun!' he roared. 'It was mine, you gave it me, she hadn't any right to break it up! Why didn't you tell her?'

'You should have stayed,' said Midge. 'Then you could have told her yourself. If you will keep running away all the time—'

'You let her! You let her break it! My gun!' Tears filled his eyes. 'I only got to play with it for five minutes!'

'I did *say*,' said Midge. 'I did *say* I oughtn't to get you one.'

'Other people have them!' Peter choked. The tears were streaming down his cheeks, dripping off his chin. 'That was the very first present anyone ever gave me and she's gone and broken it up!'

Midge felt terrible. Rashly, she said: 'Look, as soon as they give me my pocket money I'll buy you something else.'

His face brightened. 'Another gun?'

'No,' said Midge. 'I'm not buying any more guns. I could get you a book, if you like, and teach you how to read.'

'Don't want to be taught how to read!'

'But reading's *fun*.'

'I don't care! I hate it! I want my gun!'

Midge bit her lip. If only her mother hadn't had to go and *break* it. If she'd just thrown it in the dustbin she would have risked creeping down in the middle of the night and getting it out again; but a gun shattered to pieces was no use to anyone.

'Would you like a ride on my bike?' she said.

'Yes!' He grabbed greedily at it. 'I'll have a ride on your bike!'

'Do you know how to r—' began Midge, but too late: he was already up and on it.

Off down the road he shot, pedalling furiously, head bent low as if he were on a racing bike. Within seconds he was out of sight. Midge couldn't help wondering if she would ever see either Peter or her bicycle again.

Not that he would actually *steal* it; she didn't think he would do that. But he might just ride off somewhere and forget to come back. Or he might decide that as Mrs Jenkinson had broken his gun it was only fair that he should keep Midge's bicycle. Or he might—

From somewhere behind her came the sound of a bell, ringing fit to bust. She turned, and saw Peter bearing down on her.

'You're not meant to be riding on the pavement!' screeched Midge.

Peter cackled and swung out in a loop to avoid her. As he swung out he narrowly missed a parked car: as he swung back he ricocheted off a lamp post.

'Mind my bike!' yelled Midge.

'Poof!' said Peter; and, 'See what I can do!' he cried, tak-

106

ing both hands off the handlebars.

Midge could ride without her hands on the handlebars. Anybody could. There was nothing very clever about it.

What *was* clever was when people rode with their arms folded and their feet up. You needed to be really skilled for that. Midge had tried and tried but still she couldn't do it.

Neither, as he very soon proved, could Peter.

'You idiot!' screamed Midge. She dashed out into the road and snatched up her bike. 'Look what you've done . . . you've gone and ruined it!'

'It's only a scratch,' said Peter.

'It's not a scratch, it's a gouge . . . a deep big horrible *gouge*.'

'At least it's not all broken up, like my gun.'

'Oh, don't start on about your stupid gun again! You oughtn't ever to have had a gun. And anyway, I've *told* you, I'll buy you something else.'

'Not a book! I don't want a book!'

'You'll have what I get you – and don't *sulk*. Sulking's very childish.'

They walked on in silence, Midge tenderly wheeling her injured bicycle, Peter cavorting at her side.

'I'm bored,' he said, after a few seconds. 'I want to do something.'

'You've just done something!' He'd just gouged her bike. She'd have to sandpaper it before she could repaint it, and even then she probably wouldn't be able to find an exact matching colour, so that the mark would always show. 'You ought to be more careful when you borrow people's things.'

'Yes, like you were with my gun!'

They were back at the wretched gun again.

'Look, I've *told* you,' said Midge, exasperated. 'I'll get you something *else*.'

107

'I want something now! I'm bored! I want to do something! I want to play something! Let's make up a game.'

'I can't. I've got to go home and have lunch.'

Peter pulled a discontented face.

'You're always having lunch!'

'I'm not always.' She only had it once a day, the same as other people. 'Everybody has to eat.'

'*I* don't! Eating's *boring!* If you're not going to play I shall go away and play by myself!'

'So go!' said Midge.

Really, she thought, wheeling her bike, Stovey was quite right: boys *were* far more immature than girls. Boys were really quite impossible.

That afternoon, while her parents were out CND-ing, Midge went up to Sue and said: 'If I asked you, would you cut my hair for me?' Sue was good at cutting hair. It was one of the courses she was doing at college.

'You mean, really cut it?' said Sue. 'Or just trim it?'

'Really cut it.'

'Cut it short?'

Midge nodded: 'Cut it short.'

'All right,' said Sue. 'If that's what you want.' She took up her scissors and regarded Midge, questioningly. 'Are you sure it's what you want?'

'Yes,' said Midge. Stovey had said that it would suit her, and Stovey, being an artist, knew about such things. 'I'm sure.'

9

Pearl was already waiting at the station when Midge arrived there next morning. She still had on the red velvet dress which she had worn for the photographing session. Midge was wearing a sweater and jeans. (She couldn't have worn the tartan dress again even if she'd wanted, because when she'd got home yesterday for lunch she'd discovered a huge great tear in it and scrape marks on her knee, for all the world as if it had been she who had crashed her bicycle through showing off and trying to be too smart. Mrs Jenkinson had even accused her of it: 'I suppose you were riding without any hands again?' It really was quite unfair, especially as Peter, who deserved it, hadn't been hurt at all. Midge still couldn't think how it had happened.)

'Hey!' Pearl called out excitedly across the station forecourt. 'You've had your hair cut! It looks smashing.'

'So does your dress,' said Midge, generously. She noticed that Pearl was wearing bright red tights to go with it. Yesterday she had been wearing white socks.

'D'you like them?' said Pearl.

Midge nodded: she did, rather.

'It was my mum's idea . . . she says if you wear socks this weather you get a cold up your bum.'

'Really?' said Midge. When you stopped to consider it, it did seem logical. She wondered why her own mother had never thought of it.

Stovey turned up a few seconds later. Today she was all

smart and prefect-ish in a navy blue coat and white boots, so that Midge immediately felt childish and shabby, dressed in quite the wrong sort of clothes for a trip up to town and the National Gallery. But then Stovey caught sight of her and cried, 'Flora, that looks gorgeous! I told you it would suit you, didn't I?' which restored her confidence somewhat.

While Stovey went to buy tickets and look up a train, Midge and Pearl wandered over to the bookstall to see what magazines they could find. People always took magazines with them when they went on train journeys; at least, in books they did. Usually there would be a mother seeing her children off to boarding school or to stay with unknown relations somewhere remote and exciting like the Outer Hebrides, and at the last minute she would press tins of toffee and armfuls of magazines on them. Of course, the National Gallery wasn't quite the same as boarding school, and London wasn't really what you could call remote (though it was exciting) but still Midge felt one shouldn't face the journey unprepared. There was always the possibility that the train would break down and they would be stuck in the middle of nowhere for hours.

'Think I'll have this one,' said Pearl. 'It's got an article on Mick.'

Mick Matthews was one of the first year's favourite pop stars. (He sang with a group called Bedrock, whom Mr Jenkinson always referred to as Bedsock, which he seemed to think was amusing.) Pearl, clutching her magazine, went off to the cash desk, leaving Midge still picking things over. It was while she was trying to make up her mind between *Hazel*, which had good stories, and *Chix*, which was better for articles telling you how to slim without getting anorexic and letters from readers asking what to do about spots, that she became aware of someone saying 'Psst!' at

110

her from behind one of the revolving bookstands. It was Peter.

'What are you doing here?' hissed Midge.

'I want to come to London with you! What have you done to your hair? It looks horrible! I hate it.'

'Too bad!' said Midge. He didn't have to be *rude* about it. 'And you can't come to London, you haven't been invited.'

'But I want to!'

'Well, you can't.'

Peter looked mutinous. 'You can't stop me!'

'I can stop you coming with *us*.'

His lower lip began to tremble. She did hope he wasn't going to start crying again.

'Why don't you want me?'

'It's not that I don't *want* you—'

'Then why can't I come?'

Midge had the strangest feeling that they had had this conversation before.

'Because I told you, you haven't been invited,' she said.

'*You* could invite me.'

'I couldn't! It's not my treat, it's Stovey's.' She glanced over her shoulder: Stovey was just walking away from the ticket office. 'I shall have to go or we'll miss the train. I'll see you later – I'll bring you something back from London.'

'What happened?' said Pearl, as she ran back to join the others. 'I thought you were gonna buy a maggie?'

Bother. That was Peter's fault, that was. If the train went and broke down now she was going to be furious.

The train did not break down. They drank Coca Colas in the restaurant car and read the article on Mick Matthews and arrived in London just when they were supposed to arrive, which was ten minutes past eleven exactly. The National Gallery was in Trafalgar Square, which they reached by bus from Waterloo. The Gallery was very large and imposing, with double flights of steps leading up to it. Inside it was even larger and more imposing, almost like a cathedral except much busier. The first thing to catch Midge's eyes was a reassuring sign saying RESTAURANT, and, more importantly, TOILETS. (She worried almost as much about toilets as she did about having something to read.)

'We'll go there afterwards,' said Stovey, 'shall we? Unless either of you needs to go now?'

Neither of them did, so Stovey led the way up the stairs towards what she called the Bottlejerry Room. At the top of the stairs were stands selling postcards and books full of pictures, and lots of important-looking men in uniforms waiting to answer people's questions and tell them where to go. Stovey didn't need to ask questions as she already knew where to go. She had been coming to the National Gallery, she said, almost ever since she was old enough to remember. It was like Midge, and reading: Midge couldn't think back as far as a time when she hadn't been able to read, just as Stovey couldn't think back to a time when she hadn't known the National Gallery.

The Bottlejerry Room, when they reached it, turned out not to be Bottlejerry after all, but Botticelli ('Botty Jelly,' whispered Pearl, which made them both giggle). Lots of it wasn't even Botticelli but other people with foreign-sounding names, all of whom had lived centuries and centuries ago in fourteen hundred and something-or-other and painted huge big dingy paintings full of naked men with arrows sticking into them, or worse still naked women all fat and flobby which Midge could hardly bring herself to look at for fear of blushing, even though she knew that they were what Stovey called 'old masters' and great works of art. (She privately didn't think they were anywhere near as good as Stovey's painting was going to be, once it had got past the sketching stage.)

'Here's a Botticelli,' said Stovey. 'This is called *Mystic Nativity* . . . what do you think of it?'

Midge stared at it dubiously from behind her spectacles. There weren't any naked women, that was one comfort, but she couldn't say that she thought very much of the angels. There were about a dozen of them, all holding hands and wearing different-coloured nightdresses, going round in a circle in the sky. They looked as if they were hanging from a big chandelier. Some other angels down at the bottom seemed to be having wrestling matches.

'Well?' said Stovey.

Pearl put her finger in her mouth. Midge said: 'It's nice colours.'

'Yes, it is, isn't it? All those lovely rich rose pinks and that beautiful deep blue . . . I'm afraid there aren't any of my really *favourite* angels in the Gallery, but anyway that will give you some idea. Look, here's another! This one's called *Venus and Mars*. I think this one's great fun. Have a look and see what you make of it.'

Obediently they looked, willing themselves to find it fun.

'What do you think?' said Stovey.

There was a pause.

'Come on!' said Stovey. 'You must think something.'

Pearl scraped her throat.

'All them little fat things—' she said.

'The Satyrs?'

'Yeah. Satyrs . . . they remind me of Jennifer Goodchild.'

From the Botticelli Room they moved through into other rooms, lots and lots of them, all opening off one from another, with Stovey pointing out her favourite paintings and telling them what it was that she liked about

113

them. Midge's favourite was one that showed a big stripey tiger prowling through the undergrowth. At first she liked it because she thought it was called 'Tigger in the Forest', Tigger being one of her favourite characters out of *Winnie-the-Pooh*; but even when Pearl disobligingly pointed out that it was called Tiger, not Tigger, she still liked it.

'Let's go and see if there's a postcard of it,' said Stovey, so they did and there was and Midge bought it, while Pearl bought one of a circus and Stovey bought dozens of the dingy old masters and they then went back down the stairs to the signs which said RESTAURANT and TOILETS.

In the restaurant, over crisps and buns and glasses of orange juice, Stovey asked them if there was anything special they would like to do or see while they were up in London. All Midge could think of was feeding the pigeons in Trafalgar Square; Pearl wanted to see Buckingham Palace.

They fed the pigeons first – Midge fed the pigeons: Pearl wasn't too keen on it because of wearing her red velvet dress and worrying in case their feet might be dirty – then got on a bus which took them past Buckingham Palace and all the way up to Hyde Park, which Stovey said was somewhere else they ought to see. She said they would walk right across it, past the Serpentine, on into Kensington Gardens, round the Round Pond, and up to a place called Lancaster Gate where they could catch a tube back to Waterloo.

Hyde Park seemed very desolate and dreary, with the grass a mush of melted snow, and bits of ice still floating on the water. Midge wished she had some bread with her to feed the ducks and geese, but Stovey said that the ducks and geese in Hyde Park were some of the best-fed birds in the world, so that she needn't waste her time feeling sorry for them.

'Do you see any looking *thin*?' she said.

'I s'pose not,' said Midge, but she still wished she had some bread.

After they had walked round the Round Pond and were on their way to the place called Lancaster Gate, where they were going to catch the tube, Stovey suddenly said, 'I've just thought of something, Flora, which would interest you!' and tugged them both off across the mushy grass.

'There!' said Stovey. 'Do you recognize it?'

Midge stared.

'It's that statue,' said Pearl. 'That one in that book you were reading.'

Peter – it was *Peter*!

'Don't you recognize it?' said Stovey, again.

'*I* did,' said Pearl. 'I recognized it right away.'

They stood grouped round the statue. A boy with elfin locks, in raggedy clothes . . . just like Peter. *Her* Peter. Real, live, flesh-and-blood Peter . . . Midge swallowed.

'You look like you've seen a ghost,' said Pearl.

'Freezing to death, more like . . . I know I am. Come on!' Stovey gave Midge a little push. 'Time we were catching that tube.'

With an effort, Midge dragged her eyes away. Just wait until she told Peter! A statue that looked exactly like him . . .

In the train on the way home Stovey gave them their polaroids, which she said she didn't need any more.

'I've already sketched you both in . . . two lovely little angels looking as if butter wouldn't melt in their mouths!'

When they got off the train they said goodbye and thank you for taking us and 'I do hope we haven't been too much bother' (which was what Mrs Jenkinson had said that Midge had better say, 'Since you almost certainly *will* have been a bother') and Stovey went off in one direction to meet her father at his newspaper office while Midge and

Pearl went off in the other to get their bus.

'Pity you didn't come to Lorraine's party,' said Pearl. 'It was really good. She's got all these new albums we listened to.'

Midge frowned, and flicked back a plait that wasn't there. (It was funny, but they still *felt* as if they were there.)

'I had to go into town,' she said. 'Do some shopping.'

'What, with your mum?'

'No, with this boy I know.'

'Didn't know you knew any boys.'

'Course I know boys! I was talking to one this morning, wasn't I?'

Pearl looked vague.

'Were you?'

'Well, you know I was! You saw. Over by the bookstall, when you and Stovey were waiting for me. Don't you remember?'

'I remember waiting for you . . . I thought you were trying to find something to read.'

'No, I was speaking to this boy!'

'Yeah?' Pearl, losing interest, opened her magazine and gazed fondly down at the photograph of Mick Matthews. It was going to get worn out before long if she didn't stop breathing over it.

'Who did *you* think I was speaking to?' said Midge.

'Dunno.' Pearl hunched a shoulder. 'Didn't see anyone.'

'Well, considering you were looking straight *at* him you must have . . .'

Pearl must be blind as a *bat*.

Midge got off the bus in the main road. She was just about to turn down Ferris Avenue when she suddenly remembered: she hadn't bought anything for Peter. Guiltily, half expecting him to jump out from behind the nearest pillar box and demand to be 'given my present', she turned back into the main road. She would have to buy him *some*thing. He was bound to waylay her sooner or later, he was probably waiting for her even now, kicking his heels outside the back gate; he'd be terribly angry if she turned up empty-handed.

It was difficult knowing what to buy. There weren't any really interesting shops at this end of the road and in any case she didn't have very much money. She supposed she could always get him some comics – he could at least look at the pictures even if he couldn't read the words. The trouble was, Mrs Jenkinson tended to frown upon comics. She said they were full of racism and violence. Maybe sweets would be safer. All Mrs Jenkinson could say about sweets was that they rotted your teeth, and Peter's teeth weren't anywhere near the rotting stage. You could see them when he laughed, all white and sharp.

After giving the matter some considerable thought she bought him one Crunchie Bar, one Mars Bar and one Kit Kat, and set off again down Ferris Avenue, keeping her eyes peeled for any signs of hidden movement behind hedges or pillar boxes: this time she was going to be ready for him.

She was quite surprised to reach home without having been either sprung at or jumped out on. She bet he would be there waiting for her, first thing next morning.

Peter wasn't there next morning. Midge looked most carefully, both up the road and down, but there was not a sign of him. Maybe he had come and gone, too impatient to hang around even to get his present, for it was still half term and she hadn't crawled out of bed until almost nine o'clock.

As she closed the front gate a voice *did* call out, but it wasn't Peter's. Midge turned, resentfully, to see Damian Gilchrist mooning at her.

'Hallo!' said Damian.

''Lo,' said Midge.

'Are you going to the library?' said Damian.

'Yes,' said Midge.

'I thought you must be,' said Damian, 'carrying all those books.'

He beamed at her, happily, proud of his own powers of deduction. Midge shifted the books to her other hand. (If her pockets hadn't been full of Mars Bar and Crunchie Bar and Kit Kat in case of meeting Peter she could have put the books in there and then he wouldn't ever have known.)

'Would you like me to carry them for you?' said Damian.

'It's all right, thank you,' said Midge.

'I will if you like,' said Damian.

'There's only *three*,' said Midge. (And they were paperbacks.)

They walked on up the road, side by side. Out of the corner of her eye, as they passed Miss Pritchard's, Midge thought she caught a glimpse of Peter's blue jersey emerging from one of the passages, but though she turned quickly to look, there was nothing there. It must have been imagination.

'What books have you been reading?' said Damian.

'*Jo of the Chalet School, No Peace for the Prefects*, and *Give a Form a Bad Name*,' said Midge.

'Are they school stories?'

'Yes,' said Midge.

'Do you like school stories?'

'Yes,' said Midge. (She wouldn't be reading them otherwise, would she?)

'They look old-fashioned,' said Damian. 'Do you like old-fashioned books?'

'Sometimes,' said Midge. Sometimes she liked modern

118

ones, and sometimes she liked old-fashioned ones. She liked old-fashioned ones that were about girls who went to boarding school and had midnight feasts and played hockey. Girls in modern books never seemed to do any of those things.

'I like old-fashioned ones, too,' said Damian.

Midge spun round: she was sure she'd seen something blue flitting between two parked cars.

'Have you read *Tom Brown's Schooldays?*' said Damian.

Midge shook her head.

'*Tom Brown's Schooldays* is jolly good,' said Damian. 'You'd like that if you like school stories.'

She hadn't said she liked school stories about boys. (Was Peter *following* them?)

'I'll lend it to you, if you like,' said Damian. 'We've got a copy at home. It used to be my father's when he was a boy.'

'My father's got books that he had when he was a boy . . . he's got ones about Billy Bunter.'

'Yes, mine's got some of those.'

If Peter *were* following them he'd better watch out for the traffic. It wasn't safe, dodging to and fro the way he was doing.

'I don't go for Billy Bunter very much,' said Damian.

'No, I don't, either,' said Midge.

'Tom Brown is heaps better. You'd like Tom Brown.'

They crossed the main road, using the zebra crossing. (Midge couldn't help glancing back, just in case, but Peter was keeping well out of sight.)

'Which way are you going now?' said Midge.

'I'm going to the library, same as you,' said Damian. 'I want to see if they've got a book on puppet theatres.'

'*Puppet* theatres?' said Midge.

'Yes, I thought I might try to make one. They're very fascinating.'

For the rest of the way to the library, he told her about puppet theatres. Thankfully, once they were inside he left her alone, except just now and again to creep up and whisper at her.

'Have you read the Jennings books? They're about school.'

'Have you read *Swiss Family Robinson?* You ought to read *Swiss Family Robinson*.'

'Have you read *Adrian Mole*? You'd like *Adrian Mole*.'

To please Damian she took out *Adrian Mole*, and to please herself she took out *Summer Term* by Antonia Forrest and *A Little Princess* by Frances Hodgson Burnett. She had read *A Little Princess* before, but it was the sort of book that you wanted to read more than once. Damian said that he read books more than once, as well. He said that not everybody did. There were some people who read a book just the one time and then threw it away: there were *some* people who never read books at all.

Midge thought of Peter. She wondered if he really had been following them or whether it was one of those things like a trick of the light. He certainly didn't *seem* to be outside the library when she came out with Damian, though of course there were all kinds of places where he could be hiding.

'Would you like to come and have a coffee with me?' said Damian.

'I don't drink coffee,' said Midge.

'You could always have a milk shake. They do jolly good ones in Morgan's, up in the self-service. Do you ever go there?'

The last time she had been to Morgan's had been with Match and Emma, when they had looked at the lanjery and shouted about cup sizes. At least Damian wouldn't do that.

'All right,' said Midge. 'I'll come and have a milk shake.'

Over the milk shakes Damian told her more about puppet theatres. It was really quite interesting.

'When I've made my one,' said Damian, 'you can come and help me operate it, if you like. Are you any good at making up stories?'

'Yes,' said Midge.

'Could you make up a story that could be turned into a play?'

'I could make up a play,' said Midge.

'Oh, fantastic! That would be marvellous! Then we could put it on and sell tickets and get people to come and watch.'

'But you haven't made the theatre yet,' said Midge.

Damian beamed, and pushed a lock of hair out of his eyes.

'I will,' he said, '*now*.' There was a pause. 'I like your hair like that. It looks really good.'

As they were walking back down Ferris Avenue, a small figure in a blue jersey and ragged jeans suddenly dashed out from behind a parked car, shot across their path and went scuttling off down one of the passages. It was Peter. This time there could be no doubt.

'Hey!' called Midge. She ran up the road after him. 'I've got your present!'

At the end of the passage, Peter turned. Midge waved the Mars Bar at him.

'Look!'

He looked. She could see that he was tempted, but at that moment Damian arrived and almost before you had time to blink Peter was off.

'What was it?' said Damian.

Midge pushed the Mars Bar back into her pocket.

121

'Just someone I know.'

Damian stared down the passage. He seemed puzzled.

'I didn't see anyone.'

'P'raps you need glasses,' said Midge.

That night when she went to bed Midge placed the chocolate on her bedside table, along with her library books and Stovey's photographs. 'Tigger in the Forest' (she didn't care if it *did* say Tiger, it looked just like a Tigger) was up on the wall, over the mantel shelf, where she could see it when she sat up in bed. She had borrowed a piece of broken glass from the garden shed – the glass that Peter had broken when he had thrown his terrorist bomb – cut it to shape with Mr Jenkinson's glass cutter, bound it round with sticky tape and made a loop out of fuse wire. It was almost professional.

Almost, but not quite. In the middle of the night (it felt like the middle of the night, though when she looked at the cuckoo clock it was only ten past ten) Midge was woken by the sound of a crash: 'Tigger in the Forest' had slipped from the wall, landing right on top of her money box pig. She saw it the minute she switched on her bedside lamp. She saw something else, as well: the bedroom window was open, and that was odd, for it had most certainly been closed when she had gone to bed. Not totally closed, because Mrs Jenkinson had a thing about letting in the air, but only open by the teeniest little crack. Now it was gaping wide.

As she padded across to close it she thought, just for a moment, that she saw something blue gliding amongst the trees at the bottom of the garden.

Peter?

It was now that she looked at the cuckoo clock and saw that it was only ten past ten. It could have been Peter. She wouldn't be at all surprised if he spent half the night roaming about, and he was perfectly capable of climbing up the yew tree again and pushing open the window.

She peered out once more into the garden, bright and frosty in the moonlight, the trees making long black shadow fingers over the grass, but Peter (if it had been Peter) had disappeared.

Back in bed she thought that perhaps she would read for a bit, because it wasn't always easy to go to sleep again once you had been woken up. She reached out for *Adrian Mole*, which she had promised Damian she would read first, before either *Summer Term* or *A Little Princess*, and it was then that she made the discovery: the Crunchie Bar had gone, and the Mars Bar had gone, and the Kit Kat had gone. Only the wrappers remained, carelessly crumpled on the floor. Nobody but Peter would have done that.

She didn't mind so much about him climbing through the window and eating the chocolate, because after all the chocolate had been for him anyway. What she really minded was that he had torn up Stovey's photographs: the pieces were scattered on the rug, along with the chocolate wrappers. It was a mean thing to do, to tear up someone's photographs; mean and spiteful. She would never forgive him for doing that.

It wasn't until next morning that she opened Adrian Mole and discovered that he had scribbled all over the front page, but by then it didn't really make much difference. She was so cross with him already that she couldn't have been any crosser if she'd tried.

10

Peter obviously knew that he had gone too far because for the next few days he kept well out of the way. On Wednesday, it still being half term, Match called round on her bicycle and she and Midge went off for a ride together. They rode all through the back streets and up to Bethany Park, but even though she kept a sharp look-out Midge didn't catch so much as a glimpse of Peter. It was just as well, because if she had she would have said some extremely unfriendly things to him. (Just *imagine* if Stovey were suddenly to want her polaroids back and Midge had to say that they were all torn up.)

She didn't see him again all the rest of the week. It was true she didn't look for him very hard, because on Thursday she was invited next door to discuss plans for the puppet theatre with Damian, and on Friday she went to the cinema with Match and Mrs Gibbs to see *The Wizard of Oz*. Emma had been invited, but Emma apparently thought *The Wizard of Oz* was kids' stuff.

'It is, of course,' said Match, 'but *she* wanted to see it.' She jerked a thumb at her mother. 'She said she'd feel silly going to a kids' thing all by herself.'

'I said nothing of the sort!' said Mrs Gibbs. 'I said that I was going to go and that you were welcome to come if you wanted. *I* don't feel silly. I'd sooner see *The Wizard of Oz* than your stupid *Star Wars* any day of the week.'

'But you've already seen it!' said Match. 'You saw it

when you were a girl and you saw it when it was on television and now you're seeing it all over again . . . you're just being self-indulgent.'

'That's right,' said Mrs Gibbs, happily. 'Midge, would you care for some nuts or chocolate to take in with you? I don't think we'll offer my darling daughter any, she doesn't deserve it.'

On Saturday the Jenkinsons drove down to Bournemouth to spend the weekend with Grandma Jenkinson, who ran a boarding house near the sea front. It was quite late in the evening when they arrived back on Sunday, so that even if Peter had been around Midge wouldn't have seen him. She wondered if he were sulking or if perhaps he had found someone else to give him presents. Annoying though he was, she wouldn't like to think that she would never see him again.

Monday morning she went back to school after the half term break to find great excitement raging: Caroline Monahan's mother had seen a ghost, and Caroline was going round telling everyone about it.

'It's this old house that used to belong to her auntie . . . it's ever so old, it was built centuries ago. My mum always said it felt haunted. She's always had this feeling about it, ever since she used to stay there when she was a girl. She says she's always sensed things.'

Now she had not only sensed things but actually seen them as well.

'It was the same day as my mum's auntie's funeral. We'd all gone over there for it, and we'd just got back from church and my mum was out in the kitchen making a cup of tea when she suddenly saw this old lady dressed in a black shawl walking down the garden. She said it was ever so creepy, 'cos the garden's all overgrown 'cos of her auntie being too old to do anything to it, and there was this old lady all in black just walking down the path with this basket over her arm, right in the middle of all the thistles and things.'

The first years listened, eyes rounded.

'So what happened?'

'Well, all of a sudden she stopped and looked like she was opening a gate – except there wasn't any gate there – and then she started scattering this stuff out of the basket, like corn or something, as if she was feeding chickens.'

'So what did your mum do?'

'She said she just stood there, she couldn't believe it.'

'Didn't she go and say something? I would've.'

'*I* wouldn't.'

'I would! I mean, she didn't know then that it was a ghost, did she?'

'No, she thought it was just some barmy old woman that had wandered in by mistake. It wasn't till she started coming back again, down the path, that my mum went out. She said she was going to ask her who she was and what she was doing, but when she got out there the old woman just walked straight past as if she didn't exist . . . my mum said it was ever so eerie.'

'So where'd she go? The old woman?'

'She went through the back door and into the kitchen.'

'And what'd she do then?'

'She disappeared,' said Caroline.

'So how d'you know it was a ghost? How d'you know she didn't go down the hall and out the front door?'

'She couldn't,' said Caroline, ''cos we were all there. We'd've seen her. And we know it was a ghost, 'cos we've found out who it was . . . it was my mum's great-grandmother that used to live there, ages ago.'

'How d'you know?'

'How d'you find out?'

'We were looking through these old photographs,' said Caroline, 'and my mum suddenly saw this one of this old lady dressed in black with some chickens and she said "That's her!" and it turned out to be her great-grand-mother that she'd never even seen, 'cos she died before my mum was born. And my Auntie Phyllis that was there as well, she said she could remember when she was young there'd been chickens in the back garden, but my mum couldn't remember 'cos she's younger than Auntie Phyllis. But that was who it was,' said Caroline. 'It was my mum's great-grandmother, which makes her my *great*-great-grandmother, and she's been haunting the place all this time ... my mum says she always knew there was some-thing funny about it. It's one of those things that you feel.'

'Did you feel it?'

'I did that night,' said Caroline, 'when I went to bed ... I felt this sort of presence, and I knew that it was my great-great-grandmother.'

There was an awed silence.

'Wonder what she's doing it for?' said Lorraine.

'Doing what?'

'Haunting.'

''Cos she's a ghost,' said Emma. 'Ghosts always haunt.'

'Yes, but why?'

''Cos that's what ghosts do!'

'But *why* do they?'

''Cos they're unhappy.'

Lorraine looked at Caroline.

'D'you think your great-great-grandmother's unhappy?'

'Dunno,' said Caroline. 'S'pose she must be.'

'Well, of course she is!' Emma spoke impatiently. 'Stands to reason ... she wouldn't be doing it otherwise.'

In English that morning Miss Kershaw said that their project for the second half of term was to be the Edwardian era. (Emma groaned.)

'You can each be thinking of an area you'd like to

explore. Food, fashions, education ... whatever takes your fancy. In the meantime I thought perhaps we'd start the ball rolling by reading a chapter or two from *Peter Pan*. Get you into the right mood. You don't still happen to have it on you, do you, Flora. Yes?' (Another groan from Emma.) 'Oh, that's splendid! Saves going up to the library.'

While Midge was hauling her bag on to her lap to search for *Peter Pan*, Emma suddenly said: 'Caroline's mother saw a ghost the other day.'

'Did she really?' said Miss Kershaw. 'That must have been interesting.'

'It was my great-great-grandmother,' said Caroline.

'Yes, and Caroline saw her, too!'

'I didn't actually *see* her,' said Caroline.

'But you felt her – you felt her presence!'

'Yes, when I went up to bed at night and it was dark.'

'Goodness!' said Miss Kershaw. 'How spooky! Were you frightened?'

'I was a bit.'

'Tell her about it,' urged Emma. 'Tell her about your mother and your Auntie Phyllis.'

'And the garden all overgrown—'

'And the gate that wasn't there—'

'And the chickens. Tell her about the chickens!'

'All right,' said Caroline.

The class sat up, straight and proud, with an air of expectation, listening as the tale was told to Miss Kershaw. Every now and again, unable to contain herself, someone would call out excitedly, 'She had on this black shawl!' 'She was carrying this basket!' 'She was going to feed the chickens!'

'And there haven't been chickens there for *years*,' said Caroline. 'Not since my Auntie Phyllis was a girl. But my mum says she's always known the place was haunted. It's just that nobody's ever actually seen anything before.'

'Imagine seeing the ghost of your great-great-grand-mother!' said Emma.

'We reckon she's doing it 'cos of being unhappy,' said Lorraine.

'It's what ghosts do, isn't it? Go back and haunt places.'

'Specially when they've been unhappy.'

They looked trustingly at Miss Kershaw, awaiting confirmation.

'Well, since you ask,' said Miss Kershaw, 'I don't really know . . . I don't really know what a ghost *is*.'

A clamour of voices was instantly eager to inform her:

'It's a dead person—'

'Someone that's dead—'

'Come back to haunt—'

'Yes, but *is* it?' said Miss Kershaw. 'What I mean is, is it the actual spirit of someone who's dead making contact with someone who's alive—'

'Yes!'

'—or is it all part of some subconscious process that we don't yet fully understand? Suppose, for instance, that you see a picture and it makes a deep subconscious impression on you. You don't *know* that it's made an impression – in fact, in your conscious mind you might very well have forgotten all about it. But then one day something happens, like with Caroline's mother, going to her aunt's funeral, and this something triggers off your subconscious so that you suddenly start wondering why it is that you feel happy or sad for no apparent reason, or why a place you've never been to before should suddenly strike you as familiar. You've surely had those feelings?'

They nodded, dubiously, not certain what she was getting at.

'Well, if you could see into your subconscious,' said Miss Kershaw, 'you'd be able to trace a path right back through a whole chain of associations until you discovered the thing that had started it all. So maybe, when Caroline's mother saw what she thought was a ghost—'

'It was a ghost!'

'It was her great-grandmother!'

'Or was it her *memory* of her great-grandmother?'

'She couldn't have had any memory,' said Emma, 'she'd never even seen her.'

'She died before she was born,' said Caroline.

'Yes, but who knows, when your mother was a little girl and was looking through the family photograph albums, which she almost certainly would have done, she might well have seen the photograph of this little old lady dressed in black, going to feed the chickens, and in her conscious mind she'd have completely forgotten about it, but then something on the day of her aunt's funeral brought it all back to her – to her subconscious, that is. And that subconscious memory was so strong that it made her conjure up this vision. Call it imagination, if you like,' said Miss Kershaw.

A ripple of unrest ran round the room: the first year definitely did *not* like . . . .

'You mean, she only *thought* she was seeing this old woman?' said Midge.

'Quite possibly – but that makes it none the less intriguing as a phenomenon.'

It might not have made it less intriguing for Miss Kershaw: it did for the first year. Stubbornly they resisted the idea.

'Nobody could just *think* they were seeing old women walking down paths,' said Emma. 'Not unless they were bonkers.'

'It'd mean you were potty, wouldn't it?'

130

'Not at all!' Miss Kershaw spoke briskly. 'It's an excellent example of the powers of the human psyche.'

'What?'

'The *mind*,' said Miss Kershaw. 'It's quite astonishing how little we know about it.'

There was a mutinous silence.

'*I* think it was Caroline's great-great-grandmother come back to haunt,' said Emma.

'So tell me something!' said Miss Kershaw. 'Do you think if anyone else had been there in the kitchen, that they would have seen her as well?'

'Prob'ly not,' said Emma. 'It's not everyone can see them.'

'Only a few people?'

'Yes.' Emma nodded, vigorously, pleased that her point had been taken.

'And why do you suppose that is?'

''Cos only a few people are on the right wavelength,' said Emma.

'You think that's more likely than some people having such powerful imaginations that they can conjure up visions which to them seem totally real?'

'Yes,' said Emma.

'Well, there you are, it's still a fascinating subject whichever way you look at it . . . how do you feel about Joan of Arc? Were they real voices that she heard, do you think, or was it her own voice inside her head?'

Emma said they were real voices that only Joan of Arc could hear, but Match said she thought maybe they were only voices inside her head.

'So what would have caused them, do you think?'

'Fact that she was bonkers,' said Alison.

'She wasn't bonkers! She just felt very strongly about things.'

'And what about Bernadette of Lourdes, seeing the

131

Virgin Mary?'

'She was bonkers, too,' said Alison.

Match was a bit more doubtful about Bernadette of Lourdes.

'I think p'raps she just *wanted* to see something, and she wanted it so much that she made herself believe that she had.'

'So nobody thinks it was the actual ghost of the Virgin Mary come back to haunt?'

Somehow, put like that, it seemed a bit wicked. Only Emma was bold enough to say, 'It could've been.'

Match objected: 'You can't have a ghost of someone *religious*.'

'Why not?' said Emma. 'There's the Holy Chost.'

This produced another silence. It was one of those statements that nobody could argue with – especially as nobody seemed quite sure what the Holy Ghost *was*.

'That's different,' said Match, at last.

'Why?'

''Cos Holy Ghost doesn't mean ghost like that.'

'Why? What's it mean?'

'It means . . .' Match floundered, '. . . it means more like *spirit*.'

'Holy Spirit,' said Lorraine.

Emma tossed her head.

'Same thing!'

Midge, who had been thinking, suddenly said: 'Does a ghost know that it's a ghost?'

'Who can tell?' Miss Kershaw laughed, as she gathered up her books for the end of class. 'You'd better try asking one and see!'

At break time the first years split up, as usual, into their different groupings, the Icastalps (except that they weren't the Icastalps any more) huddling together by the bicycle sheds, Emma and Alison and one or two others slinking off to sit in the cloakrooms (which was strictly not allowed), Lorraine and her gang practising their passing with Caroline's netball. Match, after a bit of hesitation, had attached herself to Lorraine's lot. Midge knew that she could have joined in, if she'd wanted – Lorraine herself had looked at her and said, 'Coming?' – but Midge wanted to do some thinking, and you couldn't think in the middle of a mob. You had to be by yourself.

The best place for being by oneself, apart from hiding away in the lavatories, and lavatories were not really very good for thinking in, was over on the playing field, and especially in that furthest corner of the playing field where Midge had made her slide.

The slide had completely gone by now; there was only a bit of flattened yellow grass to show where it had been. She remembered how Peter had appeared from out of the copse and started sliding with her, showing off, being Carlotta. She remembered how she had asked him what his name was and he had said he hadn't got a name and so they had decided that she would call him Peter (and that he would call her Wendy). She remembered the day he had climbed up the yew tree, and the day they had played at bank robbers, and the very first day, when she had been sledging all by herself in Bethany Park, and suddenly Peter had been there, perched on the branch of a tree, watching her. That had been the day when he had thrown the snowball at Miss Pritchard and Miss Pritchard had thought it was Midge. Then there had been that other day—

'*Peter?*' She bounded forward into the copse: she was sure she had caught a flash of blue amongst the trees. 'Is that you?'

No reply; only the faint rustling of bare branches in the wind.

'What are you hiding for?' called Midge. 'Why don't you come out? I want to talk to you!'

Still nothing. Midge stamped a foot.

'Stop being silly, I know you're there! I shall count up to ten—'

She had reached nine before he showed himself, emerging rather sheepishly from out of the trees. It occurred to Midge that perhaps the reason he had been hiding was in case she was still cross over the photographs. She *was* still cross, of course, but not as much as she had been. She had kept reminding herself, every time she felt another burst of crossness overtaking her, that he was an orphan and didn't know any better. Graciously she decided that she wouldn't mention the photographs. But just because she wasn't going to mention photographs didn't mean he could be let off scot free.

'I hope you enjoyed the chocolate?' she said.

Peter scowled and dug the toe of his tattered trainer into the ground.

'What chocolate?'

'You know what chocolate! The chocolate I bought you – the chocolate you ate!'

'I didn't eat any chocolate.'

'So if you didn't who did?'

He hunched a shoulder. 'I dunno.'

'I s'pose you'll be saying *I* did?'

'Might've done.'

'Oh, don't be so stupid!' said Midge.

He looked at her, sullenly.

'If you're going to be horrid, I shall go away again.'

'I'm not being horrid, but it was *stupid*.' Next he'd be trying to say that it was she who'd torn the photographs up, and she who'd done all the scribbles in Adrian Mole.

'What did you want to talk to me about? If it was only the rotten chocolate—'

'No, it wasn't.' She said it hurriedly, before he could do

one of his disappearing acts. 'I was going to show you something.'

'What?'

'This.' Midge put her hand in the pocket of her duffel coat and pulled out *Peter Pan*. He eyed it suspiciously.

'That's that book you showed me before.'

'Yes, I know. But you didn't look at it properly . . . there's a picture just like you on it.'

'Where is there a picture just like me?'

'On the front. *There*.'

Jealously he snatched the book from her.

'It's not a bit like me!'

'It is,' said Midge. 'I know it is, 'cos I've seen it . . . I've seen the actual real thing.'

'What actual real thing?'

'The statue. It's up in London, in a park, and it's famous.'

There was a pause, while Peter stared down, brow furrowed, at the picture on the front of *Peter Pan*.

'I should have thought,' said Midge, 'that you'd be pleased, having a famous status named after you.'

'What are you talking about?' Angrily he threw the book to the ground. 'How can it be named after me? I haven't got a name!'

Midge bit her lip. She looked down at *Peter Pan* lying on the ground. Tenderly, she knelt to pick it up.

'Can I ask you something?' she said.

'What?'

Midge took a breath: 'Are you a ghost?'

'What do you mean, am I a ghost?' He shouted it, furiously. 'What a thoroughly impertinent question!'

'I'm sorry,' said Midge. 'I didn't mean it to be impertinent.'

'Then why did you ask it?'

'I didn't realize it would upset you.'

He glared at her.

'How would *you* feel if someone asked you if you were a ghost?'

'I don't think I should mind terribly,' said Midge.

'Then you must be totally insensitive, that's all I can say!'

What a funny word for him to use, thought Midge. She hadn't known that he knew words like insensitive – or impertinent, come to that. *She* knew them, of course. But then she read books; he didn't.

'Going round asking people if they're ghosts . . . do I *look* like a ghost?'

'I don't know,' said Midge, humbly. 'I've never seen one.'

'Well, *honestly!*'

'I'm really very sorry,' said Midge. 'Just forget that I said it.'

'How can I do that? You *said* it. It's a bit late for forgetting. You should have thought of that before you spoke. Fancy asking someone if they're a ghost! It's hardly what I should call good manners – and anyway, who could I be a ghost of? Some silly old statue?'

'No.' Midge looked down again at the book in her hand. You could only be a ghost of someone who had been alive. Peter Pan had never been alive. He was only make-believe.

'If I'd known you were going to be so rude and beastly I wouldn't ever have come back to see you, and why are you wearing those horrid tight things?'

'They're not horrid!' Midge was indignant. 'My sister bought them for me.'

'They're loathsome, I hate them!'

'Oh, you hate everything!' snapped Midge.

'No, I don't. I don't hate running, and jumping, and

things that are fun. I only hate things that are *boring*. That's
why I never do them.'

'There are times,' said Midge, in Miss Jenkinson's voice,
'when we all have to do things that are boring.'

'*I* don't!' said Peter.

'Then you'll never get anywhere in life.' That was what
her mother said: if you didn't persevere, you'd never get
anywhere. 'You'll never be anyone.'

'Don't want to be anyone! Just want to be me.'

'You'll be sorry,' said Midge.

'No, I won't! Why should I?'

'Because you won't ever have anything . . . you won't
have any money.'

'Don't want any money!'

'But you can't live without money,' said Midge.

'*I* can! You don't need money to play, and climb trees – I
bet you can't climb trees in those stupid tight things!'

'Well, I don't care!' cried Midge, vexed. 'I was the only
one not wearing them, and you can get a cold up your
bum!'

She turned and ran off, across the playing field. As she
ran she could hear his voice, mocking her: '. . . get a cold
up your bum!'

Talk about rude and *beastly*.

11

Next morning when Midge woke up she felt all fuzzy and fogged inside her head, as if the space that was normally reserved for brains had been stuffed with wads of cotton wool. The rest of her, but especially her arms and legs, seemed to have jellified overnight into some kind of heavy substance, like mud. When she raised an arm above the bedclothes it went flobbing back down with a great *thump*, and when she finally made an effort to get up her knees gave way so that she sagged in the middle like one of Damian's puppets.

Midge tottered out on to the landing and hung herself limply over the banisters.

'Is anybody there?' she croaked. (Even her voice had gone peculiar.) 'Mum? Dad? Are you there?'

Mrs Jenkinson came. She took one look and said, 'You go back to bed: I'll get the thermometer.'

On the first reading the thermometer said 105°, which was rather alarming until Mrs Jenkinson suddenly realized she hadn't shaken the mercury down. At the second attempt it only said 98.8, but even that was 0.4° higher than it ought to have been.

'I suppose we shall have to call the doctor,' said Mrs Jenkinson. 'What a nuisance!'

Midge, lying in bed like a soggy suet pudding, couldn't help feeling that it was far more of a nuisance for her than it was for her mother. Today was the day when Miss

Kershaw was going to agree the assignments for the Edwardian project. Midge had been going to suggest books. She bet now that she was away someone else would go and bag it. Lorraine Peters, probably, just because her measly aunt worked in a library. By the time Midge got back there would be nothing left but the boring subjects, like politics, that nobody had wanted – assuming, that is, that she ever *did* get back.

'You don't think I've got something awful that people die of, do you?' she said.

'Like what?'

'Like brain fever, or something?'

'Like vivid imagination, or something!'

Had she got a vivid imagination? She'd never thought about it before.

The doctor, when he came, said that he didn't know about imagination but he did know about brain fever, and one thing he could say for certain was that she hadn't got *that*.

'Just a rather nasty cold in the head.'

It seemed a bit hard, having a cold in the head, when she'd always worn her duffel coat and taken care to use the hood. It ought by rights to have been a cold up the bum. She said as much to the doctor, but he only laughed.

'I can assure you, young lady, that you would like a cold up the bum even less than a cold in the head! You just stay in bed for a day or two and enjoy yourself.'

She felt too sweaty and stuffed up to enjoy herself very much that first day. During the morning she slept, and woke again, and sniffed and snuffled; and slept again, and woke again, and gradually grew more fretful and more self-pitying (especially as she kept picturing Lorraine Peters bagging books for herself). In the afternoon Mrs Jenkinson said that she was going down the road to do some shopping.

'I'll be about half an hour . . . if the front door bell rings, just ignore it.'

Mrs Jenkinson collected her shopping bag and departed; Midge snuggled down into her pillows to doze. It wasn't the ringing of the front door bell that woke her, but the sound of tapping at the window. She knew at once what it was: Peter, sitting in the yew tree. Perhaps if she lay still and concentrated very hard she could make him go away again.

She screwed up her eyes and concentrated as hard as she could, but still he went on tapping. You'd think, if you were just imagining things—

Tap tap *tap*, went Peter, growing cross.

—you'd think you ought to be able to exercise some sort of control over them.

Tap tap *TAP*.

She would have to do something or he would start pounding so hard that he shattered the glass. Resigned, Midge heaved her suety-pudding limbs out of bed and sogged across in her nightdress to open the window.

'What d'you want?'

'I wondered where you were!' He sounded aggrieved. 'I waited for you in the same place as yesterday, and you didn't come.'

'No, 'cos I'm ill. I've got a cold.'

'I waited for *ages*. Practically the whole morning. What are you wearing that horrid frumpy dress for?'

''Cos it's a nightdress. I'm s'posed to be in bed.'

'In bed? In the daytime?'

'I *told* you,' said Midge. 'I've got this cold. I had to have the doctor. He says I'm not to go to school for the next few days.'

Peter clapped his hands.

'Goody! That means you can come and play!'

'I can't come and play, I've got to stay indoors.'

140

'What for?'

'Don't you ever listen?' cried Midge, exasperated. 'Because I've got a cold! And if I stand here much longer I shall probably get pneumonia. You'll have to go away, I'm going to close the window.'

'I don't want to go away! I want to play something! I want to play hospitals. I want to perform an operation. I want to take out someone's appendix. I want—'

'I don't care what you want!' Midge jerked crossly at the window. 'I've got a cold and I don't feel well!'

'You would if you played. If you just made a bit of an effort.'

'I don't want to make an effort! I don't want to play!'

Peter screwed up his face at her through the window.

'Why are you always so selfish?'

'*Me?*' She was outraged. 'You're just about the most selfish person I've ever known!'

Midge banged the window down; and then, as an afterthought, pulled the curtains across. When her mother came back she said, 'Oh! You're all in the dark. Why's that? Was the light hurting your eyes?'

'I couldn't sleep,' said Midge.

She might have said, 'There's a boy sitting in the yew tree pulling faces.' It would serve him right if her mother went out there and caught him. Somehow, though, she didn't think that anyone's mother ever would. If Mrs Jenkinson were to look outside now, the yew tree would be bare. Even if she had looked outside at the same time as Midge, it would still have been bare. She would think that Midge had been making it up. She might even think that she was delirious.

'How about a glass of hot milk and an aspirin?' said Mrs Jenkinson. 'That usually helps.'

Midge didn't know what time it was when Peter came back and started on his tapping again. The room was in darkness, proper night-time darkness, thick inky black without shadows, and she felt as if she had been asleep for several hours. She lay for a while, listening, then turned on her side and pulled the bedclothes round her ears. She didn't care if he did fly into a rage and pound so hard that he shattered the glass: *she* wasn't getting up to let him in.

Midge woke in the morning to find that she was feeling somewhat better. Not *completely* better, but at least more like a human being than a suet pudding. She was able to sit up in bed and eat toast fingers and a boiled egg off a tray, and put her glasses on and read *Adrian Mole* (which was quite funny, even though it was about a boy).

After she'd finished *Adrian Mole*, which was round about milk-and-biscuits time, she started on *A Little Princess*, which of course she had read before. *A Little Princess* took her up to one o'clock, when her mother arrived with a tray of lunch (tomato soup and an apple) and after lunch she read *Summer Term*, by Antonia Forrest. *Summer Term* was about girls at a boarding school doing all the things that girls at boarding schools always did, plus having rows with their sisters, which was encouraging as Midge sometimes thought that she might be the only person who ever behaved in that way.

After reading *Summer Term* she ate tea, which was peanut butter sandwiches and chocolate cake, which usually they were only allowed on Sundays on account of Mrs Jenkinson not believing cakes to be good for you – 'This is a special treat, seeing as you're ill.'

All in all, and one way and another, Midge was beginning to think that having a cold in the head was quite a pleasant sort of thing to have, the only drawback being that she had now run out of books. She had plenty of books of her own, of course, but she wasn't in the mood for reading books of her own. There were moods for reading things you'd read before and moods for reading something new and different. Now she wanted something new and different.

She could always play with her dolls, she supposed; she hadn't played with them for a long time. Perhaps that was what she ought to do.

Midge crawled out of bed and opened the wardrobe. There at the bottom, beneath the coats and skirts, all in a jumbled heap, lay IIIB. The blank gaze of Carlotta reproached her. She really ought to take them out and put them through their paces. They would be forgetting everything she'd ever taught them.

'All right, class!' Miss Jenkinson opened wide the door of the wardrobe. 'Find your seats, please, and settle down. Today we are going to learn the verb *être*, to be. *Je suis, tu es, il est* . . . Carlotta, would you care to repeat that for us?'

Miss Jenkinson looked down at Carlotta, lying on top of the pile: Carlotta looked back up at her, woodenly.

'Well?' said Miss Jenkinson; but the child remained stubbornly silent.

With a sigh, Miss Jenkinson shut the wardrobe door. People who refused to help themselves simply weren't worth bothering with.

She had just climbed back into bed and was feeling rather comfortably cosy when there was a knock at the door and Sue's voice said, 'Can I come in?'

'Knock three times and enter,' said Midge.

For once, Sue actually did as she was told. (Generally she took absolutely no notice whatsoever.) Obediently she knocked three times then stuck her head round the door.

'Guess what?'

'What?'

'I met your friend with the legs. She was on her way here to deliver this.' Sue held aloft a pale yellow envelope. 'She also gave me a Cryptic Message.'

143

'What's a crictic message?'

'One that doesn't make any sense – at least, not to me. It might to you. She said, "Tell Midge Miss Kershaw said would she do books." Does that mean something?'

'Yes.' Midge sat up, beaming, against the pillows. It meant that Lorraine Peters hadn't bagged it for herself after all. 'C'n I have my letter?'

'*Please*.'

'Please!'

'I've got something else, as well.' Sue tossed the envelope on to the bed, together with a brown paper bag. 'That's from your boyfriend. I said did he want to come in and give it to you himself, but he's too shy. He went all pink – just like you have!'

'I'm only pink because I've got a temperature,' said Midge.

'Ha, ha, pull the other one!' said Sue. 'Aren't you going to open it and see what it is?'

Midge clutched primly at the brown paper bag.

'Not with you here.'

'Oh! Pardon me, I'm sure. I shall take myself away again. *Such* a sensitive little flower.'

Sue whisked out, closing the door behind her.

'And don't try peering through the keyhole!' yelled Midge.

She waited till she could be sure that Sue really had gone, and wasn't waiting to come bursting in again, which was just the sneaky sort of thing that she was likely to do, then turned her attention to the yellow envelope and the brown paper bag. She opened the envelope first. Inside the envelope there was a card. The card said:

Ms Caroline Monahan
invites
Ms Midge Jenkinson

to
her Birthday Party
to be held on
Saturday 15 March,
at
3 p.m.

RSVP

Midge stared at it, gloatingly. Caroline had become quite a celebrity, now that she had seen the ghost of her great-great-grandmother (or at any rate felt her presence). She bet it wasn't everybody who had been invited to her party.

She propped the invitation card in a prominent position on her bedside table and picked up the brown paper bag. Inside the bag was a book. The book was *Tom Brown's Schooldays*. Inside the book was a note. The note said:

Dear Flora,

I am very sorry to hear that you have a cold. I do hope you will be better soon. I have started making my puppet theatre and wondered if you would like to come and look at it on Saturday afternoon, if you are not doing anything else, that is. Here is *Tom Brown's Schooldays* which I said I would lend you.

Yours sincerely,

Damian C. Gilchrist.

How clever of him, thought Midge, to have sent her just what she most happened to want! She settled back into her pillows to start reading.

By five o'clock, when Mrs Jenkinson came up to check how she was doing, Midge was on to Chapter Three (*Sundry Wars & Attacks*): by six o'clock, when her father arrived home, she had very nearly reached Chapter Seven.

'I thought you were supposed to be ill?' said Mr Jenkinson.

'I am,' said Midge.

'I wouldn't mind being ill,' said Mr Jenkinson, 'if it meant that I could laze around in bed all day reading *Tom Brown* . . .'

She read until her eyelids had grown heavy and were starting to droop. Every now and again she would feel them closing and would have to jerk them open again, but gradually they stayed closed for longer and longer, the words on the page became furry and blurred, and the lines of print began wandering about in a way that made it extremely difficult to concentrate. It was a nuisance, because she was really enjoying *Tom*. She really wanted to know what was going to happen next. She would have liked to have gone on reading all evening, all night, right round until m . . . .

Slowly, the book slipped from Midge's hands. Her eyelids closed, and this time they stayed closed: she would read *Tom Brown* tomorrow.

She was in the middle of a most delightful dream (in which Tom Brown and the Little Princess were having a midnight feast of condensed milk and sardines-in-tomato-sauce, together with Match and Pearl and Adrian Mole) when she was woken by a tap-tapping at the window. For a minute or so she lay there, snug in her nest, thinking cross thoughts such as *bother him*, and, *he can jolly well go away again*; and then she felt mean, because he was an orphan and didn't know any better, whereas she'd been invited to Caroline Monahan's birthday party and was going to go and look at a puppet theatre and was reading *Tom Brown*, and it didn't somehow seem quite fair, and so in the end, with an air of martyrdom, she wriggled out of bed and went to let him in.

'But you can't stay long and you'll have to keep quiet

'cos my parents are downstairs watching television and they'll hear you if you start making a noise.'

'They won't hear me!' Boastfully, he vaulted over the sill. 'People only ever hear me when I want them to. Like when I *shout*—'

'Don't!' hissed Midge.

'Or when I *jump*.' In one flying leap he was across the room, landing squarely in the middle of the bed. 'This is fun!' He bounced experimentally. 'Like a trampoline! *Up* to the ceiling and *down* to the floor, and *up* to the ceiling and—'

'Stop it!' said Midge. He was doing it even more vigorously than Match had done. 'You'll break the springs!'

'Stop it!' squeaked Peter. 'You'll break the springs . . . silly old nanny! Why didn't you let me in last night?'

''Cos I was asleep.'

'All *night?*'

'People do sleep all night,' said Midge.

'*I* don't. I don't sleep ever. Sleeping's a waste of time. What's this?' He had stopped trampolining and was investigating the contents of her bedside table. Jealously he picked up Caroline's invitation. 'It's got flowers on it!'

'That's 'cos it's an invitation to a party,' said Midge.

'What party?'

'Someone's birthday party. Girl in my class.'

'I want to come!'

'You can't,' said Midge. 'It's only girls.'

'Why is it only girls? What a stupid thing for it to be!'

He flung the card angrily to the floor. As Midge stooped to retrieve it, the thought occurred to her that maybe the party *wasn't* going to be only for girls – maybe there would be boys there as well. She wouldn't actually mind if there were boys; not if they were like Damian. But Peter still couldn't come, because he hadn't been invited.

'What's this silly book with all these silly-looking people on it?'

'It's not a silly book, it's *Tom Brown's Schooldays.*'

'*School*. Eeugh!' He tossed the book from him. 'What d'you want to read about *school* for?'

'I like reading about school.'

'School's *boring*. What's this?'

That was her note from Damian. She snatched it from him.

'It's private!'

'Why? What's it say?'

'It's a private letter.'

'Who's it from?'

Midge coloured slowly.

'The boy that lives next door.'

'*That* soppy idiot?'

'He's not soppy!'

'You said he was. You said you hated him. You said—'

'Yes, I know,' said Midge. 'That was before I got to know him.'

Peter scowled, rather ferociously.

'So what does he do now that makes him not soppy?'

'He likes reading,' said Midge. 'And he's making this puppet theatre and I'm going to help him. I'm going to go round there Saturday and I'm going to write a play, and we're going to put it on and make programmes and invite people to come and see it and—'

'I don't want to hear about all that!' Peter sprang up, impatiently, from the bed. 'Stop talking about things that are boring and let's *do* something ... let's play something!'

'I can't play now,' said Midge. 'I've got to go to sleep.'

'*Again?* You went to sleep last night!'

'That's what nights are for,' said Midge. 'And anyway, I've got this cold and if I don't get enough rest it won't get better.' And if it didn't get better she wouldn't be able to go round to see the puppet theatre.

'You sound like a mother,' said Peter, disgusted. ' "If you don't get enough rest, it won't get better." '

'Well, it won't,' said Midge.

'Poof!' He pranced across to the wardrobe and wrenched open the door. 'Where are the dolls? I want to play with the dolls! Which is this one? Is this the stupid one?'

'No, that's Carlotta. Put her back.' Firmly, Midge took Carlotta away from him, stuffed her back into the wardrobe and closed the door. 'We can't play dolls now.'

'But I want to!'

'Well, you can't.'

For a moment she thought he was going to go off into one of his sulks, or even throw a tantrum. She could see that he was considering it, but then at the last minute he obviously changed his mind and decided on a different tack.

'*Please*, Wendy, can't we?' he said. 'Just for five minutes? *Please?*'

It was very difficult to resist Peter when he coaxed, for he could smile very nicely and blue eyes were always appealing, but she knew that she must. It had been fun staying at home for just one day reading books, but now she wanted to be fit for going back to school and playing hockey, and going round to Damian's, and Caroline's party.

'I'm sorry,' she said, 'but it's far too late, and I really don't feel like playing with dolls any more anyway.'

His face darkened.

'What do you mean, you don't feel like playing with dolls any more?'

'Well,' Midge rubbed a finger up her nose, 'there are so many other things to do ... I haven't really got the time.'

'You had time before!'

'Yes, I know.'

'So why haven't you got time now?'

Midge was silent.

'What you really mean is that you've grown out of it! That's what you really mean, isn't it?'

She supposed that it was.

'You're just like all the rest!' shouted Peter. 'Growing out of everything that's any fun!'

'I didn't *want* to grow out of it,' said Midge. 'It's just something that happened.'

'That's what they all say! And then they get old and boring.'

'I'm not getting old and boring, but—' Midge suddenly remembered Miss Kershaw '—one can't be a Peter Pan for ever.'

'What are you talking about?' He demanded it querulously. '*I* can. I can be Peter Pan for just as long as I like. I shall be Peter Pan for always and always!'

For always
    and always
        a
          n
            d
              a
                l
                  w
                    a
                      y
                        s
                          .

150

'Midge?' Her mother was suddenly in the room. 'What are you doing out of bed? Have you been having a bad dream, or something?'

Midge shook her head.

'And why are you still wearing your glasses? I hope you haven't been reading all this time!' Mrs Jenkinson reached out to take them off. 'Now, whatever is the matter? You're not crying, are you?'

Midge sniffed, and wiped the back of her hand across her nose. Of course she wasn't crying! She was going to write a play for Damian's puppet theatre, wasn't she? She was going to go to a birthday party, she was going to do books for her project. What was there to cry for?

That's what they all say! And then they get old and boring . . . .

Peter wouldn't get old and boring. He would be Peter for ever and ever. And there would always be another Wendy, somewhere, for him to play with.

He had probably gone off right now to look for one. And if anybody were to ask him, 'Do you remember that Wendy with the pigtails and the glasses who gave you a gun?' he would look completely blank and reply, 'No. Who was she?'

He wouldn't remember her as she would remember him.

'You do know that it's nearly ten o'clock,' said Mrs Jenkinson, 'don't you?'

'Yes.' Midge crept back into bed and pulled the clothes up to her chin. 'If I haven't got a temperature tomorrow,' she said, 'can I go back to school?'

'We'll see,' said Mrs Jenkinson. 'Maybe, if you get a good night's sleep, without any more disturbances.'

There wouldn't be any more disturbances. Peter wouldn't be coming back again to tap-tap at the window and be let in. And if by any chance he did—

But he wouldn't. This time, she knew, he had gone for good.

'I've just remembered,' she said, 'I've *got* to go to school tomorrow, we've got a hockey match.'

First years against second, and Stovey was going to referee. She didn't intend to miss *that*.

More Beaver Books

*On the following pages you will find some
other exciting Beaver Books to look out for
in your local bookshop*

BEAVER BOOKS FOR OLDER READERS

There are loads of exciting books for older readers in Beaver. They are available in bookshops or they can be ordered directly from us. Just complete the form below and send the right money and the books will be sent to you at home.

☐	WATER LANE	Tom Aitken	£1.95
☐	FRANKENSTEIN	David Campton	£1.75
☐	IN THE GRIP OF WINTER	Colin Dann	£1.99
☐	TWISTED CIRCUITS	Mick Gowar	£1.75
☐	FANGS OF THE WEREWOLF	John Halkin	£1.95
☐	TEMPEST TWINS Books 1 – 4	John Harvey	£1.99
☐	YOUR FRIEND, REBECCA	Linda Hoy	£1.99
☐	REDWALL	Brian Jacques	£2.95
☐	THE GOOSEBERRY	Joan Lingard	£1.95
☐	WHITE FANG	Jack London	£1.95
☐	ALANNA	Tamora Pearce	£2.50
☐	A SHIVER OF FEAR	Emlyn Roberts	£1.95
☐	A BOTTLED CHERRY ANGEL	Jean Ure	£1.99
☐	THE MAGICIANS OF CAPRONA	Daina Wynne-Jones	£1.95

If you would like to order books, please send this form, and the money due to:
ARROW BOOKS, BOOKSERVICE BY POST, PO BOX 29, DOUGLAS, ISLE OF MAN, BRITISH ISLES. Please enclose a cheque or postal order made out to Arrow Books Ltd for the amount due including 22p per book for postage and packing both for orders within the UK and for overseas orders.

NAME ....

ADDRESS ....

....

Please print clearly.

BEAVER BESTSELLERS

You'll find books for everyone to enjoy from Beaver's bestselling range—there are hilarious joke books, gripping reads, wonderful stories, exciting poems and fun activity books. They are available in bookshops or they can be ordered directly from us. Just complete the form below and send the right amount of money and the books will be sent to you at home.

☐ THE ADVENTURES OF KING ROLLO	David McKee	£2.50
☐ MR PINK-WHISTLE STORIES	Enid Blyton	£1.95
☐ THE MAGIC FARAWAY TREE	Enid Blyton	£1.95
☐ REDWALL	Brian Jacques	£2.95
☐ STRANGERS IN THE HOUSE	Joan Lingard	£1.95
☐ THE RAM OF SWEETRIVER	Colin Dann	£1.99
☐ BAD BOYES	Jim and Duncan Eldridge	£1.95
☐ MY NAME, MY POEM	Jennifer and Graeme Curry	£1.95
☐ THE VAMPIRE JOKE BOOK	Peter Eldin	£1.50
☐ THE ELEPHANT JOKE BOOK	Katie Wales	£1.50
☐ THE REVENGE OF THE BRAIN SHARPENERS	Philip Curtis	£1.50
☐ FENELLA FANG	Ritchie Perry	£1.95
☐ SOMETHING NEW FOR A BEAR TO DO	Shirley Isherwood	£1.95
☐ THE CRIMSON CRESCENT	Hazel Townson	£1.50
☐ CRAZY SEWING	Juliet Bawden	£2.25

If you would like to order books, please send this form, and the money due to:
ARROW BOOKS, BOOKSERVICE BY POST, PO BOX 29, DOUGLAS, ISLE OF MAN, BRITISH ISLES. Please enclose a cheque or postal order made out to Arrow Books Ltd for the amount due including 22p per book for postage and packing both for orders within the UK and for overseas orders.

NAME ....

ADDRESS ....

....

Please print clearly.

JOAN LINGARD

If you enjoyed this book, perhaps you ought to try some more of our Joan Lingard titles. They are available in bookshops or they can be ordered directly from us. Just complete the form below and enclose the right amount of money and the books will be sent to you at home.

☐	MAGGIE 1: THE CLEARANCE	£1.95
☐	MAGGIE 2: THE RESETTLING	£1.95
☐	MAGGIE 3: THE PILGRIMAGE	£1.95
☐	MAGGIE 4: THE REUNION	£1.95
☐	THE FILE ON FRAULEIN BERG	£1.99
☐	THE WINTER VISITOR	£1.99
☐	STRANGERS IN THE HOUSE	£1.95
☐	THE GOOSEBERRY	£1.95

If you would like to order books, please send this form, and the money due to:
ARROW BOOKS, BOOKSERVICE BY POST, PO BOX 29, DOUGLAS, ISLE OF MAN, BRITISH ISLES. Please enclose a cheque or postal order made out to Arrow Books Ltd for the amount due including 22p per book for postage and packing both for orders within the UK and for overseas orders.

NAME . . . .

ADDRESS . . . .

. . . .

Please print clearly.